THE TRAIL TO RECLAMATION

PLAINSMAN WESTERN SERIES BOOK EIGHT

B.N. RUNDELL

The Trail to Reclamation
Paperback Edition

Wolfpack Publishing
5130 S. Fort Apache Rd. 215-380
Las Vegas, NV 89148

wolfpackpublishing.com

Paperback ISBN 978-1-63977-256-8
Large Print Hardcover ISBN 978-1-63977-257-5
eBook ISBN 978-1-63977-255-1

As I write this, it's the end of May in the mountains of Colorado, and it's snowing. We have over a foot already and more coming down. The white stuff blankets the land with beauty and silence, muffling the usual sounds of life. This has been a difficult time for my family, my wife lost her mother and my last brother also passed from this life. But even with heaviness in our hearts, there's also joy in the wonders of the Lord. So, it is with a special appreciation to my Lord and my God, that I say thank you! Thank you for all you have done through the years for me and my family and friends, thank you for the opportunity to share my thoughts with so many around the world, and thank you especially for your gift of eternal life. It is because of that, that I will one day be reunited with so many family and friends, never again to part.

Thank you.

THE TRAIL TO RECLAMATION

1 / SEASONS

The wind whistled as it tossed the snow about. It was springtime in the Rockies, but high up in the mountains spring was slow in showing its colors. Reuben Grundy was struggling to get to the lower pasture where the horses needed feed, but the old snow had crusted over, and the new snow was doing its best to blind and aggravate the tall, lanky man. His hat was pulled low, his collar turned up, a scarf wrapped around his neck, but his long blonde hair still whipped at his face, slapping ice-tipped locks across his cheeks and into his eyes. Each step was a fight, the crust thick enough to hold him until he placed all his weight, just shy of 200 pounds, on each stride and he would crash through the icy edges and sink to his waist and more. He had to get to the horses, for they were having the same difficulty pawing away at the crusty ice-capped drifts, trying to get to water and the few sprigs of grass that were fighting for sunlight.

The morning sun winked through the blowing snow, casting shadows across the icy hillside that was framed by tall pines with humbled branches bearing white clumps. Reuben's first glimpse of the horses showed them huddled at the lean-to shelter on the uphill side of the meadow. The long-eared pack mule stood guard, his head hanging beside the body of the long-legged blue-roan gelding known as Blue that had been Reuben's faithful ride for several years. Beside the roan and pushed up close was the leopard Appaloosa mare of his wife, Elly Mae, and the bunch was completed by a buckskin gelding and a blood sorrel mare, recent additions to the herd. The last of the grass hay was crowded into the far corner, the tarp covering stretched tight to keep the animals from scattering the lean remains.

When Reuben made it to the pole fence, only the tops of the posts showed clearly, but some of the top rails showed thin lines above the deep drifts that marked the boundary of the wide meadow covering almost ten acres surrounded by spruce and ponderosa pines. Long shadows stretched into the meadow, the icy crust sparkling with diamonds of sunlight tinted pink from the rising sun that blushed its way above the low foothills framing the big valley spreading wide below the flanks of the Sangre de Cristo Mountains. The same mountains that marched like uniformed sentries coming from the northwest to the southeast, each bearing dark blue shoulders dusted with winter's last snow while boasting glistening white plumed helmets that crested the now hidden granite peaks.

Reuben drove the handle of the double-bladed axe deep in the drift as he struggled to break through the drifts and surmount the rail fence. As he dropped to the far side, he was waist-deep in the drift, fighting to make progress. He was bound for the narrow stream that came from the spring above the cabin, but the cold had covered it with thick ice and drifting snow. Finally reaching the stream, he kicked at the snow, uncovering the icy crust, and began hacking away to give the horses access to the thin stream that gurgled underneath.

A bray from the mule brought Reuben's head up as he twisted around to look at the huddled horses and mule at the lean-to shed. The mule stood, butt to the shed, ears up, nose pointed, as he let loose another tree-shaking bray. The big blue roan had come to the side of his friend and with head high and ears pricked, he pawed at the snow, but looked at the fence line below the towering ponderosa. Reuben turned his attention to the north fence that showed in the shadows of the tall trees. With the slow rising sun stretching shadows, it also bent its morning lances of gold into the meadow, showing moving shadows that flitted through the trees, orange eyes flaring in the dim light, but watching the animals within the fenced pasture.

"Wolves," growled Reuben, fighting the wooden buttons on his buffalo coat trying to get to his Remington Army .44 caliber revolver from his hip holster. As he dug for his pistol, he started toward the horses, keeping his eyes on the wolves, but struggling with the drifts. With most of the meadow blown clear, once he was free of the drifts he started at a dogtrot toward the shed, but the wolves were padding over the crusted snow and had made it into the meadow.

The leader of the pack, a big black, started his stalk, undoubtedly unnerved by the braying mule and now with head down, teeth showing in a snarl, the scruff of his neck standing and eyes blazing. With a growl over his shoulder, he commanded his pack and each one moved to the side, assuming the same attack stance, and they moved together, glaring at the horses and ignoring the lumbering creature to the side. The beasts growled, snapped their jaws, and moved closer, now about thirty yards from their quarry.

Reuben held the axe in his left hand as he lifted the Remington and took aim at the leader. He squeezed off his shot, not missing a step, forcing his way to stand between the wolves and the stock. The bullet blossomed red, and the leader stumbled, bit at the annoyance at his shoulder and turned his attention back to the mule. The Remington bucked again and the grey wolf at the near side of the leader fell to his chin, twisting at the wound that showed red on the grey fur. The grey wolf whimpered, lying on its side, feet pawing the frozen ground, trying to right itself. Another blast from the pistol and the leader fell to its shoulder and the others turned their attention to Reuben. With a glance to their downed leader, the remaining two wolves turned their attention to the man and as if on command, they snarled and charged.

Reuben snapped off another shot at the leader of the two, but before he could fire again, they were on him. The first had blood on his chest, but the second showed teeth as its weight bore Reuben to the ground. The animal snapped and snarled, biting at the uplifted arm, but the thick buffalo coat protected Reuben's arm as he pushed against the attacking wolf. Suddenly the wounded wolf sunk his teeth in the thick fur of the sleeved arm that had held the axe which now lay on the ground where it fell when the wolves drove Reuben to the ground. Both beasts were biting, ripping, and tearing at anything they could get their teeth into. Reuben protected his face, but the mad beast tore and pulled, exposing Reuben's face to the attack of the wounded wolf.

But the charge of the bloodied grey ended when the

beast was catapulted into the air, kicked by the angry mule, both rear hooves launching the attacker into the deep drift. With his left arm free, Reuben stuffed his mittened fist into the mouth of the remaining wolf, driving him back as he fought with the man. Reuben struggled to his feet, the teeth of the wolf sinking into the mitten that had been fashioned from the hide of another wolf at another time. But the wolf was unrelenting and as he pushed against the man, Reuben stumbled back just as the mule sunk his teeth into the flank of the wolf, taking a hunk of fur and hide from the beast.

The wolf released his bite on the mitten, turning to face the new threat, and dropped into an attack stance facing the mule. The mule lifted his head, ears standing tall, and stretched out his neck and let loose a long, ear shattering bray, that sounded like he was laughing at this furry creature that dared to come at him. As the wolf took one tentative step, growling and snapping at the mule, the meadow was filled with the roar of a rifle blast and the fur of the wolf blossomed red as the animal was sent tumbling to the side to fall into the icy snow, painting it red.

Reuben snapped around to see his wife, Elly, standing at the fence with her smoking Henry rifle, searching for another target. But all the attackers were down, unmoving and the nervous horses came to the side of their protector mule, looking from Reuben to the wolves. Reuben chuckled and started toward Elly, "What took you so long?"

"So long? When I heard the first shot, I grabbed my coat and the rifle and started out in your tracks! It's a good thing you broke trail otherwise I'd still be fighting the drifts and you'd be breakfast for them wolves!" she declared, grinning, and nodding to the downed beasts.

Reuben made it to the fence, kicked away some of the drift to give him a place to stand and leaned back on the top rail to look at his beautiful blonde wife. He smiled and said, "It sure is good to have a protector. Don't know how I'da made it this long without you watchin' o'er me!"

"Ain't that the truth. Looky there, that nice, thick buffalo coat, them wolf-hide mittens, that hand-knit wool scarf, they did more'n keep you warm, they kept you alive!" she giggled, smiling at her tall, blonde, broad-shouldered love.

"Ummhmm, we make a good pair, don't we?"

Elly smiled, shook her head, and asked, "Ummhmm, but tell me, what'd you contribute to this," motioning to his get-up, "protective armor?"

Reuben grinned, shaking his head, grunted, "Humph, I kilt this buffalo," grabbing at his heavy coat, "an' I kilt these wolves," waving the gloves at his daring wife and laughing.

"But I skinned 'em, tanned the hides, sewed 'em up, and fitted 'em to you. That takes skill. All you did was pull the trigger!" she chuckled, turning to look at the horses. "And since I pulled the trigger, you might wanna get them carcasses outta the meadow so the horses can get to the water and such. They don't like the smell o' them wolves and all that blood!"

"You sure are gettin' bossy! Am I gonna hafta turn you over my knee again?"

"Again?! You ain't done it the first time, and just so you know, there ain't gonna be a first time!" she laughed, turned, and started away, calling over her shoulder, "Better hurry, breakfast'll be ready soon!"

Reuben chuckled, shaking his head, and returned to his work. He picked up the axe and went to the water hole to finish making a big enough hole for the horses, and large enough to keep from freezing quickly. Once done, the animals that stood watching and waiting, stepped closer and dipped their noses in the icy water to drink their fill. Reuben went to the lean-to and stripped off the tarp and scattered about half the remaining grass hay and retied the tarp over the rest. With that done, he started at the task of dragging the carcasses of the wolves out of the meadow.

After dragging the big black leader from the meadow, he started back for the others. When he returned with the second wolf, he was surprised to see Elly already at work skinning out the black. She looked up at him, "Didn't want 'em to freeze 'fore we could skin 'em out. It's easier now!" she explained, without stopping.

Reuben grinned, shaking his head at the wonder of this woman, and returned for the others. When all four were in the trees, Reuben slipped his skinning knife from the sheath at his belt, preferring the smaller knife to his Bowie that hung at his back. He dropped to one knee beside the carcass and began to strip its hide. Within a short while, the experienced pair had finished with the skinning and had rolled up the hides to pack to the cabin. Reuben looked at Elly, "You go ahead back to the cabin, I'll drag these carcasses away and be there shortly."

"Breakfast is ready, so don't take too long!" declared Elly, picking up one of the bundled hides and turning to the cabin with just a glance over her shoulder to give Reuben a coy smile.

2 / SUPPLIES

"If we're gonna make Canon City 'fore dark, we need to get a move on!" declared Elly, looking across the table at her handsome husband as he leaned back in the chair, sipping the last of his coffee.

"Now, don't get in such an all-fired hurry, woman! I need muh coffee, you know that!" responded Reuben, grinning at his wife through the rising steam from the hot coffee.

"Well, how's about you get a move on and get those horses and that mule up here so we can get on the trail while the sun's shinin'! I don't cotton to bustin' snow drifts down through that canyon along Grape Creek after dark!"

Reuben chuckled, "What'chu fussin' about. You never hafta bust drifts, that's me'n Blue's job!"

Elly giggled, picturing the long-legged blue roan pawing at the deep drifts, and buckin' through them, belly dragging on the icy crust and Reuben sittin' atop with wide eyes and a fearful expression. "If we're lucky, that warm sun that's finally peekin' outta them clouds will make those drifts retreat into the trees. After all, it's the first of May and the flowers wanna come outta hibernation and decorate the hills and they can't do that with snow drifts everywhere."

"Well, we've had a few warm days, all except this mornin', and it's lookin' bright out there now, so, I reckon it'll be alright," answered Reuben, sitting down the empty coffee cup and rising from his seat. He went to the door, plucked his coat from the peg and snatching his Henry from the rack above the coats, he glanced back at Elly, "I'll be back in a few minutes, but don't hold your breath!"

"Oh, you make me breathless all the time," giggled the pert little blonde, casting a coy smile to her husband. They had been together just over two years, but the many adventures and excitement they had known made it seem like they had been together most of their lives. It was hard to remember life without each other, and neither would want to know it. Elly turned, hands full of the morning dishes, to the counter and the pan of dish-water. Her mind drifted to the previous years from the time they first met when Reuben rescued her and several others from the Sioux. They had been traveling with a wagon train when the Sioux hit and captured the women, and it was Reuben who became the sole rescuer. But that encounter led to them becoming husband and wife, united in a joining ceremony by the leader of the Arapaho people, Little Raven.

Before their chance meeting in the plains, Reuben had been a member of Berdan's Sharpshooters in the early days of the Civil War, but after being wounded and his brother killed, he was mustered out and began his westward trek. When they helped recover some stolen gold taken from the stage line, Ben Holladay of the Overland Stage used his connection with the governor of Colorado Territory to get both Reuben and Elly appointed marshals to help protect the stage shipments. Yet after some challenging assignments, they had become disenchanted with the job and were determined to return the badges and leave the marshal's service, but that had not been completed yet.

It was just a short while when Reuben returned riding Blue and leading Elly's appaloosa mare, Daisy, and the pack mule. He slipped to the ground, tethered the three animals at the hitchrail below the porch and mounted the steps to retrieve the gear to rig the animals for their journey to Canon City for supplies. He hauled out the saddles, blankets, bedrolls, panniers, packs, parfleches, and more and began rigging the three animals. Elly soon joined him and started saddling Daisy as the appaloosa turned her head and nudged the woman. Elly chuckled, rubbed Daisy's head and cheeks, stroked her neck. "I know, I know, I've been neglecting you, but I still love you!" she declared, still rubbing the appy's neck.

Reuben watched, smiling, and remembering the girl he first met as a captive of the Sioux. She and the others were trying to keep up their courage, but it was evident they all were scared to death, but Elly, or Eleanor as she was known then, showed a stiff upper lip and belligerently stood up to her captors. When Reuben handed her a Henry rifle, she wasted little time using it, killing one of the captors and wounding another. When the dust had settled, he remembered thinking she was not just a beautiful woman but one that would stand beside her man and for the first time in his life, he began thinking about having a woman at his side. Now he grinned, knowing that the decision to take her as his wife was probably the best decision he had ever made.

It was mid-morning under a wide blue sky and warm spring sun they started on the trail taking them through the rugged foothills down to the settlement of Canon City. It was a town originally laid out and started as a supply point for the burgeoning goldfields in South Park. The mines were busy and producing millions of dollars' worth of gold for the growing nation, and supplies were needed for the bustling area. With a good road and access, Canon City became a prominent commercial center for mining and would one day be a processing center with many smelters. Oil had also been discovered and the wells provided kerosene and fuel oil. But now, all Reuben and Elly wanted was enough supplies to see them through the coming summer.

The sun was dropping behind them and casting long shadows as they came from the canyon of Grape Creek and approached the banks of the Arkansas River. The spring snowmelt had yet to raise the water levels and they found it easy to make their crossing with the gravel bottom providing good footing and the water level not yet belly deep. Once across, the horses paused and shook, rolling their hides to shake off the excess water, making Elly grab the saddle horn and giggle as the appaloosa did her number.

They approached the bustling burg from the west, riding in the shadows of the long line of hogbacks and started down the main street where the assortment of buildings ranged from a few stone or brick buildings to several smaller lap sided wood structures. They turned into the livery and smithy, left their horses and mule for the night, and with bedrolls, saddle bags, and rifles in hand, walked across the street and entered the McClure House, the only semblance of a hotel available. They had stayed there before, remembering the expressed vision of Mrs. McClure, of wanting to build an "honest to goodness, fine hotel." But for now, it was little more than a spacious house with several spare bedrooms and a short path to the outhouse.

"Well, I need to wash up before we go anywhere! I've got dust from head to foot, even with the muddy, drift covered trail, somehow, I've managed to collect all the dust between here and the valley!" declared Elly, lifting the pitcher of water to fill the basin at the washstand.

"Well, don't use all that water, I need a little washin' too!" answered Reuben, sitting on the edge of the bed and bouncing to test the springs.

Elly had never been one to primp and pamper herself, but she did take a little pride in her appearance. With her beaded buckskin tunic and leggings over her high-top moccasins, she could pass for an Indian maiden if it weren't for her fair complexion and long blonde hair. Reuben was outfitted in a similar fashion, but his buffalo coat and her wolfskin coat covered their outfits until they stepped through the door to Ma's Café.

"Well, look what the cat drug in!" declared a smiling and buxom woman everyone called Ma. She recognized the pair from previous visits and was always glad to see them visit again. "So, comin' outta the mountains to resupply are ye?" she asked, grabbing the big coffee pot and a pair of cups as Reuben and Elly seated themselves at the table nearest the front window. The lowering sun was sharing the last of its golden lances, bending them through the window to showcase the dust that danced in the thin air.

"That's right, Ma!" answered Elly.

"But it's really your cookin' that brought us down here!" declared Reuben.

"Oh, pshaw! I know better'n that. Why, this little whip of a girl can cook ever bit as good as me, I reckon. You're just sufferin' from cabin fever and needed to see some fresh faces!" She smiled and framed her face with her hands as she looked at the pair. "Got sumpin' special in store, do ye? That cantankerous ol' telegrapher, Halstead, was in here askin' 'bout'chu. Said he got a telegram from the gov'nor's office for you."

Reuben looked at Elly, shaking his head and breathing deep, lifting his shoulders. They had been appointed deputy marshals at the urging of Ben Holladay and Marshal Moses. It was at a time between governors and at the behest of the incoming new governor, Evans, for help in protecting the shipments of gold from the goldfields. But after a bad experience the previous summer and fall during the Indian uprisings and the massacre at Sand Creek, Reuben and Elly had determined to resign, but the governor went to Washington to campaign for a senate seat, leaving Colorado Territory without a governor. Reuben shook his head, "I guess we'll need to check that out come mornin' when the telegrapher opens his office. After all, we are technically still marshals," he shrugged.

"Fine! But let's have a meal in peace first! It might be the last peaceful one we have for a while," grumbled Elly. She looked up at Ma, "What's the special, Ma?"

"Got some fresh beef! Had some cows come in 'fore

winter set in and the rancher sold me a couple. Been eatin' on 'em ever since. Made a fine mulligan stew!"

Elly smiled, glanced at Reuben and back to Ma. "Sounds great! We'll both have that!" she declared, smiling at both Ma and Reuben who was nodding his agreement.

3 / PLANS

"Ain't never had no telegram from the gov'nor's office afore!" stated the grinning telegrapher, Halstead. He chuckled as he handed the envelope to Reuben.

With a nod to the telegrapher, Reuben turned, glanced at Elly and they walked from the office onto the boardwalk. A bench sat in front of the office window, and they seated themselves as Reuben tore open the envelope and began to unfold the telegram.

Office of the Governor, Territory of Colorado

Deputies Grundy,

Have report from Ft. Garland of influx of settlers and prospectors. Fear the increase in numbers will rile the Ute and Apache. Need civil authority to contain. Go at once. Your jurisdiction will cover southern Colorado Territory. Gov. Evans gone to Washington, new governor to be appointed. Current territory marshal, Uriah B. Holloway agrees.

Theodore W. Moses, U.S. Marshal, Western District, Mo.

"Well, there you have it!" grumbled Reuben, dropping

his hands to his lap, still clutching the wrinkled telegram. He turned to face Elly, shaking his head, "What do you think?"

"The way they act, ain't nobody else in the entire territory!" mumbled Elly, shaking her head and looking up the street to see the awakening town and the beginning bustle of the residents and businesspeople. Somewhere a screen door slammed, a rooster crowed, and the rasping squeak of a water pump heralded the coming awake of the community.

"Whaddaya mean, ain't nobody else?" queried Reuben.

"You know, nobody else that can keep the peace, round up the bad guys, and such," grumbled Elly.

"Well, we weren't quite sure what we were goin' to do, so..." answered Reuben, grinning as he shrugged.

Elly elbowed him, giggled a little and added, "Well, if we're gonna, we better get our supplies and git goin'!" She stood and offered Reuben her hand to help him up from the low bench. He chuckled, stood, and followed her lead down the boardwalk to Morgan's Emporium. As they neared, Elly turned to her man, "Maybe you could go get the horses while I start buyin' our supplies?"

"There ya go, orderin' me around again," grumbled a grinning Reuben.

"Well, somebody's gotta do it. You don't want some old maid, or grumpy old man that smells like a buffalo, doin' it, do ya?"

"Nope," chuckled Reuben, stepping off the boardwalk to cross over to the livery.

The trail from Canon City followed the winding path of Grape Creek. The trail cut through the juniper and piñon covered foothills where Grape Creek had long ago carved its route through the rugged terrain, leaving behind a steep walled canyon that scattered dark shadows along the creek bottom and trail. Leaving the confluence of Grape Creek and the Arkansas River, the trail sided the creek on its circuitous route into the western mountains. If it were to travel a straight line, the trail would be half the distance, but the stubborn mountains pushed it around each finger ridge that jutted into the canyon, making it easier traveling, but longer by miles. They had traveled about six or seven miles, when the mountains seemed to lower their shoulders and offer some mid-day sun for the travelers. The creek was enjoying the first of the spring snowmelt and would soon be cresting its banks, but for now, the warm sun was welcome as it brought comforting warmth to their shoulders and backs. Reuben reined up, motioned Elly to do the same, as he stepped down, stretching his legs, and let Blue take a drink of the icy water. As he arched his back, he looked at the neighboring peaks, noting the one known as Horseshoe Mountain and the taller Tanner Peak on the opposite side of the creek.

Elly noticed his frown as he shaded his eyes and looked at the crests of the snow-covered peaks and asked, "What's bothering you?"

He dropped his hand and looked at Elly, "Don't like those cornices at the top of those peaks and the steep slopes of the canyon."

Elly frowned, shaded her eyes, and looked toward the maw of the canyon they were soon to enter. She knew the north winds were notorious for blowing the snow over the crest of ridges and the tips of the peaks, making overhanging cornices of icy snow that resembled glaciers. But those glaciers had poor footing and with lighter snow underneath, the heavy cornices were held in place only by the freezing temperatures. When the warm sun of spring dropped those temperatures, the cornices would crumble and if the terrain was steep and the snow deep and heavy, an avalanche would clear the slopes of snow, trees, and rocks, destroying everything in its path.

Elly looked at Reuben, "Think we can make it?"

Reuben shaded his eyes again and slowly shook his head, "Prob'ly. It's early yet, haven't been too many warm days, and it's cold higher up, so..." he shrugged. He took a deep breath that lifted his shoulders and reached for the rein of his ground tied Blue and looked over his shoulder at his woman, "Let's get through there 'fore it lets loose!" He swung back aboard his horse and glanced at Elly, "You take the lead. I'll watch the mountains, you watch the trail!"

Elly nudged Daisy past the big blue roan and started on the trail that rode the bank of the creek, often pushing willows and chokecherries aside. There was snow on the trail and the animals walked quietly, feeling the tension of their riders, and often looking down the trail and up at the steep slopes that held the deep snow. It was about a half-mile through the lower foothills where the shoulders of the lower mountains held scattered scrub juniper and piñon and bunches of scrub oak brush. But the lower hills gave way to the steep sided towering peaks. Although not as high and rugged as those that stood above timberline, they were rugged none the less with shadowy talus slopes, rocky escarpments, and narrow declivities that scarred the steep sided peaks. Yet it was a white canyon that beckoned them on, whispering the invitation as a ghostly ogre summoning strange interlopers to their deaths, holding wide arms outstretched with pointed shoulders that seemed anxious to shrug free of winter's cloak.

Hooves whispered along the trail that rose from the creek bottom to a narrow shelf carved into the talus slopes on the north of the canyon. With the south side soaking up the sun and sparkling white, the breeze whistled off the steeper north walls, the icy tentacles tugging at the scarf laden necks. Reuben kept Blue close behind the appaloosa of Elly, often shouldering the rump of the smaller mare, but reassuring Elly of his nearness. He spoke softly, "If anything breaks, let Daisy have her head but keep her moving as fast as possible. It's just a little over a mile further on, but…" he was interrupted by the loud crack that came from high above. It sounded louder than a rifle shot, but Reuben knew instantly what happened. The cornice at the crest had broken off and would be driving the mass of snow down. He shouted, "NOW! GO!" and grabbed his hat and slapped it on the spotted rump of the mare.

The little mare lunged and dug hooves deep in the snow as Elly leaned forward, laying low on the horse's neck. Reuben dug heels to Blue and was soon close behind the mare. The long lead of the mule was taut, but Reuben knew the mule would not be left behind and without a glance backward, he knew the animal was close. The crack of the cornice was so loud, the report bounced across the canyon and was soon echoed by another from the south rim. Reuben glanced to his left to see the wide, heavy cornice at the crest of the taller peak break off, almost in slow motion, peeling itself free from the peak and marching itself like a monstrous plow pushing the snow below. It blossomed into a billowy white cloud and began to thunder its way down.

But the roar to his right jerked Reuben around to see the massive cloud of white surging down the steep chute between the razor-edged ridges that seemed to be guiding the deadly avalanche to the trail below. He looked ahead to see the black tail of the appaloosa lifted high and the clinging form of Elly, laying low on the neck of the mare, probably encouraging the horse onward. Reuben slapped legs to Blue, leaning forward, his hands almost reaching the ears of his horse as he too shouted, "Go boy! Go! We gotta make it!" as he continued slapping his legs to the ribs of his four-legged friend.

The roar came from both sides of the canyon as the two avalanches raced one another to the bottom. The wind carried the loose snow like the banshee of a blizzard, whipping about the canyon and searching for any weakness or living creature to torment. The horses stretched out their necks, noses with flaring nostrils, manes whipping in the wind, feet digging into the uncertain footing of the hanging trail. Reuben saw the big shoulder of granite overhanging the trail at the end of the long ridge and knew if they could make that, they would be safe. He shouted to Elly, but his voice was drowned out by the roar and the echoes. He wasn't certain, but it seemed there were other avalanches starting, all because of the thunderous rumbles that were charging down the steep slopes. The first clumps of snow flitted across the trail, making Reuben dare to look above at the overwhelming whiteness that rose as a billowy monster reaching to consume all below. He leaned forward, "Go Blue! You can do it!" he hollered into the mane of the roan. He felt the gelding reach further, dig deeper, and lunge ahead just as the big mule made a desperate leap to escape the first of the massive icy boulders. In an instant, they were swallowed by the dark shadow of the granite boulder overhang, to hear Elly yell, "Whoa!" as she jerked the appy to a stop, only to be run into by the big roan. All were soon stopped, sides heaving, as Elly and Reuben twisted in their saddles to see the cascade of ice and snow thunder over the trail and crash into the creek bottom, rapidly filling up the gorge with its cargo.

Elly looked at Reuben, back to the snow, shaking her head. She was breathing heavy, and her hands were shaking as she grabbed at the saddle horn and Daisy's mane to steady herself. She leaned down, buried her face in the mare's mane and rubbed the animal's neck, "Oh girl, you did so well! Thank you, thank you, thank you!" She twisted to the side, saw Reuben doing much the same, stroking Blue's neck and speaking softly to the big gelding. Reuben swung down, but as his feet hit the ground, he grabbed at the saddle horn to steady himself, chuckling as he looked at Elly, "Whoa! My legs gave out! Whoooeee!"

"If it's alright with you, I'd just as soon get outta this canyon before I get down!" answered Elly. She reined Daisy around, took the trail and nudged the mare away from the overhang and into the light. Reuben followed, grinning, but grateful.

4 / JOURNEY

After a warm night in their cabin, they set to and readied everything for their planned journey to Fort Garland. They talked into the night about what lay ahead for them and agreed it would be best to get the story of the incursion of settlers and prospectors into the San Luis Valley direct from the commandant of the fort.

"But what will we do about the other horses? We can't leave them corralled up, that just makes them an invitation to more wolves and bears!" asked Elly, always the one concerned about the welfare of those around her —man and beast alike.

"I thought about that. I reckon we can just let 'em run free, leave the gate open. They did it before, last summer, if you remember. That way they can take shelter in the lean-to if they want or find grass and water wherever they may. Most animals tend to stay close to home, so I reckon we can find 'em when we return," suggested Reuben, standing to turn into the cabin, stretching and yawning to make his point.

"But...do you really think they'll be alright?" questioned Elly, standing to follow her man into the cabin.

"Elly, you know I would do anything I can to take care of all the animals—you, the horses, that mangy dog, Bear," nodding to the big black dog lying near the door, catching the fresh air that came in under the door and lifted his head as if he knew they were talking about him.

Elly turned to Reuben, frowning, "Mangy? He's not mangy! He's a good dog and he's saved your bacon a time or two!" she fussed, shaking her little fist at the grinning man.

"I know, I know. But if it's alright with you, I'd like to turn in cuz we got an early start tomorrow and lots to do before we pull out!"

The mule was packed with two panniers, two parfleches, a large haversack, and spare blankets. It was a typical load for the big mule, but he rolled his hide just to settle the pack saddle into place. He turned to look at Reuben, pointing his long ears at the man as he lifted one corner of his upper lip and snarled at the man as if dissatisfied with his load. Reuben slapped the grey beast on his rump, "That's alright mule, you've carried heavier loads before!"

Reuben looked at the doorway to see Elly coming out, carrying her bedroll under one arm, her Henry rifle under the other. She was outfitted in her usual attire, a long buckskin tunic, beaded and fringed by the Arapaho women that made it for her, buckskin trousers, fringed at the side seams, and tall beaded moccasins. Her wolf-skin coat lay across her saddle and she quickly slipped the Henry into the scabbard, tied her bedroll behind the cantle, and lay the coat atop the roll. Her saddlebags carried extra ammunition, her medical kit of bandages and salves, ointments, and more, plus mittens and other incidentals.

Reuben was outfitted much the same, choosing his wool capote instead of the heavier buffalo coat. He carried both the Sharps and Henry rifles, each in its own scabbard on either side of the saddle. His saddlebags also carried extra ammunition for his rifles and powder and caps for his pistol as well as his binoculars and other accouterments. Reuben looked at Elly, "Ya ready?"

"Ummhmm, but I'd rather be stayin' and puttin' in that garden you promised two years ago when we built this cabin!" she grumbled, smiling to lessen the blow.

"Maybe soon," he answered, swinging aboard his big blue roan. He watched as Elly made a quick hop, jammed her foot in the stirrup and swung her leg over the rump of the appaloosa and settled into her saddle. She nodded to her man, smiled, and watched as he reined around and started to the saddle of their timbered hills, to take the trail south down the miles-long Wet Mountain Valley.

"Think we'll see any of our Jicarilla Apache or Mouache Ute friends?" asked Elly as she rode beside Reuben. She watched the big dog, Bear, scouting well out in front, often stopping, and looking back to be sure they were following. They were staying on the high east side of the valley, shouldering the low rising foothills that separated this valley from the distant valley of the Arkansas River. With the warming temperatures of spring, the lower reaches of the wide basin, although always deep with grass, would be soft bottomed, with the ground thawing and the sub-irrigated land hiding deep, black dirt bogs that could swallow a heavy-laden horse or mule. Snow was melting in the higher mountains and usually dry creek beds would be carrying that runoff to the thirsty bottomland.

"Doubt it. Since they were here last season, they'll be campin' elsewhere this year. They usually rotate summer camps to let the graze and game replenish 'fore comin' back. But I'll be happy as long as we don't run into them consarned Comanche!"

"You!? I'd be happy to never see another Comanche! Those few we saw last summer o'er Fort Lyon way were bad 'nuff, but when they took us women captive the summer before that..." she shook her head at the memory, thankful for her man that rescued them. Yet this was the land where it all happened, and the trail they would take from this valley would be the same the Comanche had taken the captive women—and she was not anxious to relive that experience.

"Well, this'll be a three-day trip and we'll cut from that trail soon as we can. I reckon we'll camp near Muddy Creek after it breaks from the valley, from there we'll go across the Huerfano River and on to that crossing they call the Sangre de Cristo Pass, then drop into the valley and be at the fort."

"Would you look at that!?" declared Elly. She had twisted around in her saddle to look at their backtrail and now sat, shading her eyes with her hand, looking behind them.

Reuben turned to look and saw two horses, a buckskin, and a sorrel, trotting with tails up, manes flying, following their trail. They were the two horses they left behind, but with the gate open, they had decided to join the others in their journey. Reuben shook his head and looked from the horses to Elly, "That don't surprise me. Every time I worked with them, they always crowded close to the others never wanting to be separate from them. Guess we'll just hafta let 'em follow."

"But…" began Elly, looking at the horses coming at a trot. They were obviously happy and determined and enjoying the freedom and the new country. "What if…"

"What if what? They might come in handy. We could use 'em as spares, extra pack horses, whatever. Maybe even make a trade with 'em." He lifted his shaded eyes to the sun, noted it was nearing mid-day and pointed to a cluster of juniper, "How 'bout we take a break, stretch our legs."

"Sounds fine to me," answered Elly, turning to look at the two additions to their remuda.

PASS CREEK WAS NOT MUCH OF A CREEK, BUT WITH THE beginning of spring runoff, it was showing more water than usual. Reuben and Elly had followed the trail that shouldered the creek almost to its headwaters before making camp at the end of the second day of travel. They were a little higher than the valley bottom as was evidenced by the abundance of tall ponderosa, spruce, and fir that made up the almost black timber that grew so thick on the flanks of the higher mountains. These were the mountains that skirted the Sangre de Cristo and even though towering and rugged, they were nothing more than a teaser of the bigger peaks of the Sangres. They made camp where the creek hugged the black timber and clung to the chokecherry and kinnikinnick that were just showing some buds, ready to burst out in bloom with the warm spring sun.

Even though they had seen a passel of game, elk, deer, and even a few antelope, they were using up some of the elk meat that had been kept in the basement cooler and was tender and tasty. The strips were sizzling over the flames, the coffee pot was dancing, and the frying pan snapped and popped with fresh cattail sprouts gathered along the lower reaches of the creek while the Dutch oven was doing its business under the layer of hot coals resting on the lid and underneath the pot's legs. Reuben leaned back against the log, Elly sat on the log beside him, and he looked up at her, smiling, "This is great! The smell of pine, the cool, clear air, supper smellin' fine, and a beautiful woman beside me – it don't get any better!"

Elly playfully slapped his shoulder, smiling, and said, "It is nice. I love the mountains and just the two of us together. This is what we always talked about when we first were together."

"Ummhmm, 'til Holladay got involved!" grumbled Reuben, his face painted into a frown. He was remembering when he and Elly had retrieved a stolen shipment of gold for the Overland Stage company and the owner, Ben Holladay, was so glad to get it back, he convinced them and the territorial marshal to make them deputies so they could protect future shipments of the gold going from the goldfields in South Park and being shipped to Washington for the war effort. That was the beginning of their stint as deputy marshals, and since that time they had put in their duty in many different ways and places.

"And so it continues. Is this time going to be much different? I mean with outlaws, Confederate renegades, Indians, and so on?" questioned Elly.

Reuben chuckled, looking up at his woman, knowing that every time he looked at her, she seemed to get even prettier than before. "Prob'ly not. But if we keep at it, we might get the whole shebang territory straightened out, and then you can plant your garden!"

"Well, then, you better get right on that, sweetheart!" she answered, rising to check the steaks and the rest of their supper.

5 / FORT GARLAND

With hands clasped behind their heads, they had snuggled under the blankets and took a moment to stare at the stars. It had become a common practice when sleeping in the wilderness, always taking time to enjoy the beauty and wonder of God's creation. "That's a screech owl!" whispered Elly, smiling in the dark as they listened to the nearby bouncing call of repeated short hoo-hoos. He was answered by a higher pitched warbling call that almost sounded like a whistle.

"Ummhmm, and that's his lady friend answering," replied Reuben. "Hear those coyotes?"

"Kinda hard not to, they are makin' a racket, that's for sure. Sounds like mama's bringin' home the food for the young'uns!"

"Ummhmm, but those red-winged blackbirds over there," nodding to the scrub oak, "need to shut up and go to sleep," grumbled Reuben.

The high-pitched squeal and booms of the nighthawk seemed to put a period to the sentence of night sounds, but the sudden quiet was unsettling and unnatural. Both Reuben and Elly appeared to hold their breaths, listening to the whisper of the night breeze in the pines. He looked to the horses to see Blue standing, head high, ears pricked and nostrils flaring with the mule beside him also attentive to the darkness. Bear had come to his feet, a low growl coming from his deep chest and his scruff standing tall. He took one tentative step toward the open park that lay on the far side of the creek and paused, one foot lifted as his head dropped into his attack stance. Reuben slowly rolled from his blankets and came to his feet in a crouch with his Henry in his hands and held across his chest. He stared into the starlit night, squinting to look at the willows and chokecherries that lined the creek, seeing the movement of a shadow.

"Somethin's at the far side of the creek," he whispered with a glance to see Elly also in a crouch with her Henry.

"I see it, but it looks like there's more'n one," she answered in a low whisper.

A pine squirrel scolded them from the tall branch of a ponderosa, unafraid of whatever had alarmed the others. At the sound, the shadows stopped, apparently listening, and waiting. A loud squeal sounded, repeated, and was answered by a series of low grunts that echoed across the wide park. Reuben chuckled, looked at Elly, "Sounds like a mama bear and her cub or cubs."

"That squeal sounded like a little pig!" declared Elly, relaxing and standing tall as she craned to look at the shadowy figures on the far side of the creek.

"I don't think they'll try to cross the creek, she prob'ly just brought 'em from the den and lettin' them explore a mite."

"Them? You mean there's more'n one?"

Reuben nodded, "Looks like it." The mama black bear was padding away, two rolling shadows, still squealing a mite, were doing their best to keep up.

"Ohhh, they're so cute when they're little!" mewed Elly, grateful for the waxing moon peeking from behind the clouds to light the way for the night travelers.

"Yeah, they're cute – when they're over there and we're over here. But don't get caught between the mama and her young'uns, cuz she'll tear you up!"

"I know, I know," answered Elly, leaning her rifle against the log that shielded their blankets and dropped to her knees to crawl back into the warm covers.

THE RISING SUN WAS OFF THEIR LEFT SHOULDER WHEN THE trail joined the rough wagon road that came from the east. They pointed their horses to the west, staying on the road that shouldered the headwaters of the Sangre de Cristo Creek and split the notch that took them through the low range of timbered mountains at this break in the Sangre de Cristo Range. After about another ten miles, the road took to the broad shoulder that flanked the high peaks of the mountain range. But they chose to stop for nooning on the banks of the Sangre de Cristo Creek.

With Blanca Peak catching the midday sun and its snowcapped tresses shining bright, it seemed to light the way into the broad expanses of the south end of *En Valle de San Luis.* They chased the sun across the shoulder, dropping back to the banks of the creek as the road entered the wide valley and showed the clustered buildings of Fort Garland. Without any walls or stockade, the wood and adobe buildings were arrayed around a central parade compound with a tall flagpole displaying the banner of stars and stripes. As the sun settled onto the western mountains, Reuben and Elly rode into the fort, stopping at the hitchrail of the Sutler's and stepping down.

"Let's check in with the commandant, if he's in," suggested Reuben, turning to the building on the south side of the compound. He glanced to Elly as they walked to the commandant's office, "Last time we were here, it was a Colonel Tappan, but I reckon with the war and such, there's somebody else in charge now."

As they neared the door to the office, a man stepped out, turning to pull the door shut and turned to face the couple. "Well, hello! Were you coming to see me?" asked the uniformed man. He was a tall man, the dark blue uniform with shiny brass buttons and gold braided epaulets marked him as an officer and the twin bars on his shoulder told his rank of captain. He started to put his hat on but deferred when he looked to Elly. "Ma'am."

"If you're the commandant, yes," explained Reuben.

"I am that. Please, join me," he offered as he opened the door and stepped back inside.

Reuben allowed Elly to go before him and the two joined the captain in the interior office as he walked behind the desk and seated himself, motioning for them to be seated in the chairs before the desk.

Reuben held the chair for Elly, then seated himself as the captain began, "So, what can I do for you folks?"

"We are Reuben and Elly Grundy, deputy marshals assigned to this territory. I understand you wired the governor's office because of the influx of so many settlers and some prospectors?"

The captain frowned, looked from Reuben to Elly and back, "Both of you are deputies?" he asked, with a tone of incredulity.

"That's right," answered Reuben, remaining stoic but

with a glance to his wife who was grinning a little mischievously.

The captain fidgeted a little in his chair, picking up some papers and shuffling them to the side. He looked at Reuben, "Yes, well, I've become somewhat concerned as we see more and more wagons coming into the valley. There have been some that plan on continuing west to join the California trail, but I'm not sure they'll do that. Most are looking for land to settle on or gold they can dig. What with the rush on the gold fields north of here, I think most of 'em have the idea that Colorado territory is covered with gold that will make 'em all rich. But the natives are none too happy about all these white men invading what they see as their home lands. Now some of 'em have agreed to move to reservations, but others, well, they're not willing to give up their homeland, and I can't say as I blame 'em."

"So, is most of the problem between the white men and natives, or just the blue and the grey?"

"A little of both. The original location of the training for rebel recruits was just over those mountains," nodding to the mountains northeast of the fort, "and there's still some that think they can keep the war goin' out here. But, I'm thinkin' it'll all be over and done 'fore the year's out, so..." he shrugged, looking up at Reuben from under his thick single brow.

"As far as the natives, which tribe and who is the potential powder keg?" inquired Reuben.

"The Tabeguache Ute under Ouray are the friendliest, they signed the Treaty of Conejos and gave the land east of the Continental Divide to the white man, but he's been peaceful. But the Mouache and Capote, well, they're not happy with Ouray and Kaniache, although he's been a friend of Carson, he's not anxious to make peace. The Jicarilla Apache, who can tell?"

Reuben looked at Elly, back to the captain, "We've known Kaniache, and he can be stiff necked alright, but all in all, he's a good man. But when it comes to conflict with prospectors, the gold seeker doesn't seem to care much for the native that might be keeping him from his rich strike he's been dreaming of, and most are willing to kill any native that gets in their way."

"The reason I asked for civilian authority, was for the conflicts between the prospectors and settlers and maybe some of the problems with the natives, if you're obliged, but we can deal with most of the natives, especially after they hear about Sand Creek!" declared the captain, letting a grin paint his face.

Reuben and Elly frowned as Reuben asked, "And what do you know about Sand Creek?"

"Well, we showed 'em then, didn't we?" chuckled the captain.

"Yeah, the army showed the native that anything in blue are a bunch of lyin', murderin' animals!" declared Reuben, rising and taking Elly's elbow in hand. "We were there, captain, and we *know* what Chivington did and all he did was start a war with the natives that will cost more lives than you can count!"

The captain stood, holding his hand out to stop them, "Whoa, whoa, hold on there! I didn't mean to upset you! I was just going on what I heard. But we can't let that come between us, we've got to work together here."

Reuben paused, turned to look at the officer, nodding. "You're right, captain. It's just that we lost some friends there, and friends of friends, women and children alike. But maybe we can do something to keep that from happening again."

"Good, good. Now, there are quarters for you at the end of the officers building. It's got a good stove, and everything you might need. The sutler will have anything else. You're welcome to make this a base for your work, if you like. That way, we can keep each other apprised of happenings."

"That would be good. Thank you, captain," answered Reuben. "And if you'll excuse us, we need to put our horses away and get settled into our 'base'."

"And if you would like, join me in the dining hall in, say, an hour?" invited the captain.

"That will be fine, captain. Thank you."

6 / SURVEY

The officer's table in the mess hall was filled with Captain Kerber, Lieutenant Edward Jacobs, Assistant Surgeon F.R. Waggoner, and Reuben and Elly. After the meal was served, Reuben looked to Captain Kerber, "So, captain, just where are all these prospectors and settlers you were concerned about?"

The captain chuckled, reached for his coffee, and looked at Reuben, "Purt near anywhere in the entire valley! But most of 'em have gone to the northwest foothills, a few went west along the Rio Grande, and some are on the west face of the Sangres. But there's new ones comin' all the time. Some from the east o'er the pass, some from the south through Taos an' followin' the *Viejo Sendero Español* or the Old Spanish Trail laid out by ol' Rivera and then de Anza. But the few I talked to seem to think this is like South Park where all the strikes were in the lower reaches of the mountains on the west edge of the park. Now as to settlers, well, most o' them are on the southwest parts, some along the Rio Grande and I heard of some in the north end. Course, there's Carson's brother-in-law, Tom

Boggs, he's done a little ranchin' further up the Rio Grande."

"So, just about anywhere, huh?" responded Reuben, glancing to Elly and back.

"Would you want an escort, marshal?" asked the young lieutenant. "I've wanted to do a little more exploring of the area and it would be good experience for us."

"Well, that's tempting, lieutenant, but if we're going to meet up with any of the natives, they get a little spooky around soldiers," responded Reuben, glancing at Elly as she gave a slight nod to show her agreement. "And as for the white men, some of 'em might resent the blue and not be very cooperative either," added Reuben.

Elly leaned forward, reaching for her coffee, and looked at the captain, "As far as the natives, we know the Jicarilla are in the south, and the Ute are basically in the west, but are you aware of any particular encampments?"

"I'm still new here at Garland, but what some of the old-timers tell me, the Ute have their summer camps usually along the Rio Grande, while the Apache most often stay south of the big river in the foothills, but they move around and now that spring is showing up, some of them, both Apache and Ute, might be on the move to other hunting territory, maybe even go to the eastern plains after some buffalo."

Elly glanced to Reuben, "And run into the Kiowa and Comanche and maybe even some Arapaho."

Reuben nodded, sipped his coffee, thinking. With a glance to Elly, he turned to the captain, "We might just make this our base, but we're more used to bein' on the move. We'll let you know when we leave and where you might find us...*if* we're needed. But we'll prob'ly make a scout of the valley, get to know the land and such, maybe talk to any settlers or others. Sometimes it's enough for people to know there's law in the area to keep 'em in line."

Their attention was turned when an enlisted man came charging into the mess hall, looked around and spotting the officers, stepped quickly to the side of the captain, snapped a quick salute and handed the captain a telegram. He grinned as he watched the stern face of the captain relax into a smile as he read the gram and looked around the table, "Good news! Lee surrendered to Grant at Appomattox!" he declared loudly enough to be heard throughout the mess hall. A sudden cheer and shouting broke out among the soldiers and servers.

Reuben looked at the captain, "Does that mean the war's over?"

"No, not completely. Although Lee was the highest-ranking officer of the confederacy, he only commanded the Army of Northern Virginia, a force of about 30,000. But there are others, like Johnston's Army of Tennessee and Nathan Forrest and his cavalry, and others. No, I think it'll be a while 'fore it's all over." He paused, looking at the telegram and looked up at the others, grinning, "But this is a great start! Hopefully our nation will get back to livin' instead of fightin'!"

"Amen to that!" declared Reuben, reaching for Elly's hand.

The captain frowned, "Did you serve, marshal?"

"I did captain, I was one of the first with Berdan's Sharpshooters. We did a lot of fightin' till I took a couple lead balls," he touched his upper chest at the memory, "and was mustered out after that. Lost my brother to the fighting and the rest of my family to some renegades posing as the home guard."

"Did they pay?" asked the captain, already assuming he knew the answer.

"They did, captain. Every one of them."

AS THEY RODE FROM THE FORT, ELLY LOOKED BACK AT THE adobe structure that shown white in the early morning sun. She twisted around in her saddle, looked at her man with a smile, "It's a bit different, us travelin' with just a pack mule trailin' behind us and not those two yearlings."

Reuben chuckled, "Well, I talked to the hostler at the livery 'bout them, he seemed to think he might be able to get a good price for them. He says there's always folks comin' through that need a good horse and they could bring a premium."

"I was kinda fond of that little sorrel."

"She was a good 'un, alright. But she might still be around when we get back if you wanna keep her."

"It's not that, I'm content with Daisy here," leaning forward to stroke the mare's spotted neck, "I just liked the little girl. That blood-red color and the flaxen mane, and those stocking legs, she was purty!"

"Ummhmmm, but when they get too purty, others get to likin' 'em and one day they come up missin' and end up tied off at some buck's tipi," chuckled Reuben. They were riding almost due west, making for the Rio Grande that came from the mountains beyond the flats, but shouldered up against the smaller foothills on the south end of the big valley before it bent to the south and made its way to the big waters. The sun was at their back and gave a little warmth in the cool spring morning. High overhead a golden eagle screamed at them, ducking his head to look for his breakfast they might kick out of the brush.

Ute Creek and Sangre de Cristo Creek came to a confluence with Trinchera Creek where the larger creek had a wide bend to the west. It would ultimately converge with the Rio Grande but for now the lower wetland offered a respite from the dry sagebrush and cacti-covered flats. The wagon road on the Old Spanish Trail that was primary trail used by settlers stayed atop the flats while the creek cut its way west, carving a wide arroyo to make its way, leaving the scar across the dry flats. A dry gulch offered an easy access to the rippling creek and the greenery that rode the banks. Reuben motioned to the creek and led the way into the bottom of the defile.

He stepped down, caught the rein from Elly as she slid to the ground between the horses. The mule pushed his way between the willows and the appaloosa to get his drink as the horses dipped their heads to the water. Elly looked at a backwater, saw a growth of cattails and said, "I'm gonna get some sprouts for our dinner," and worked her way to the marsh to make her gather. Using the tail of her tunic, she soon had her armload and started back to Reuben, but paused as he motioned her quiet, nodding to the high bank of the arroyo.

With binoculars in hand, Henry hanging from a sling, Reuben quickly mounted the steep, rocky bank and slipped up to the edge to take his look-see. Less than a hundred yards away a large band of natives moved to the east. With heavy-laden travois and horses, the band included families with their hide lodges. Reuben guessed there to be a village of maybe thirty or more lodges. Elly whispered, "Who are they?" and her presence startled him. He frowned, lowering his binoculars, and whispered, "What are you doing?" and twisted around to look at the horses. The animals were tethered to the willows and stood secure, but he shook his head and grinned at his woman.

"You always leave me behind! I wanted to see too!" she whispered, grinning.

"Prob'ly goin' east to the plains for some buffalo. I think they're Ute, but I don't see any familiar faces.

"Let me see," responded Elly, reaching for the field glasses.

They were hidden behind a scattering of sage and buffalo grass but could easily see the moving band. "Maybe they're the Tabeguache under Ouray or Shavano."

"Maybe, the captain did say Ouray was a little more peaceful and prone to make a treaty," replied Reuben. "Maybe they're goin' to the fort to see the captain."

"Maybe, but for now, we'll have to wait 'em out 'fore we leave here," exclaimed Elly.

7 / INCURSION

Although the caravan seemed to be the epitome of confusion and chaos, the band of Ute was the plains example of efficiency. Able to move an entire village within hours, the experienced travelers functioned as a single unit, everyone doing their part and within the course of a day, could move the village many miles and never miss a meal or an opportunity for a hunt to provide game for the families. As the dust settled behind them, Reuben slipped down the rocky slope of the arroyo and gathered the horses and mule, checking their rigging and making ready to resume their journey.

The sun was well up but still behind them as they topped the bank of the Trinchera and turned west. His landmark was a cluster of pointed buttes just north of the creek but about five miles distant. He turned to Elly, "Maybe we can make our noonin' when we get to those buttes," pointing to the west. From the distance, Elly thought them to be no more than big anthills, shaped the same and covered with the same buffalo grass, rabbit brush, and scraggly greasewood and sage as the rest of the valley.

Bear was leading the way but often left the trail to chase after one of the many long-eared jackrabbits that were so plentiful and fast enough and cagey enough to keep from getting caught by the big wolf-looking dog. After another disappointing chase, he would return to the trail, tongue lolling and head hanging, but always willing to resume his scout in front of the small group of travelers.

The trail stayed atop the north shoulder of the creek, keeping well above the marshland that marked the meandering stream. While the creek wandered from one twisting streambed to another, it always left behind wider marshes marked by water lilies, cattails, and timpsila. Whenever Elly spotted a good growth of timpsila, she looked for the dusty purple blossoms and would mentally mark the location for a return when the tubers were big and ripe. For now, she would gather the shoots of the cattail, some wild onions, and maybe some blue camas.

They stopped between the buttes and the creek, dropping down to the sandy bank beside the creek to let the horses and mule drink and to have fresh water for coffee. The sun was high and bright, giving more warmth than wanted for there was little shade near the creek save for a small patch on the lee side of a stand of juniper. With a small fire near the junipers, they made a pot of coffee and ate the cornmeal biscuits from the early breakfast at the fort. A short snooze, a good rest for the animals, and they were back on the trail.

When the sun nestled in the western mountains, golden arrows were launched skyward by the setting orb bidding its last goodbye to the warm spring day and Reuben and Elly found their campsite under a cluster of cottonwoods that populated a peninsula that jutted into the big bend of the *Rio Bravo del Norte* or the Rio Grande River. After their first sighting of the Ute village on the move, they had seen little sign of any white man incursions, save for one burnt out wagon and the skeletons of a couple mules which had probably been from the previous summer.

Reuben pulled the coffee pot back from the flames, dropped in a handful of ground coffee and dropped the lid back to give it time to brew. He looked up at Elly who was spearing several strips of meat onto the willow withes for broiling. She saw his look and asked, "Two of these gonna be enough?"

"Better make it three or four, I'm so hungry my belly button's pinchin' muh backbone!" he chuckled.

She giggled as she shook her head, not pausing in her work. She had already put the Dutch oven with corn dodgers atop the coals and shoveled some hot coals on the lid to bake them through. The hanging pot was suspended from the tripod of thin saplings and the bubbly concoction of leftover meat with timpsila, onions, and cattail shoots, was letting them know it was going to be ready soon. Their camp was well-protected with thick, tall willows, chokecherries, and kinnikinnick —the leafy cottonwood that overhung the fire would dissipate the smoke. Their bedrolls were stretched out underneath the trees, gear stacked nearby, and horses and mule picketed between their camp and the water, giving them plenty of graze and water. Bear lay beside Elly, hoping for a scrap which was offered occasionally, and the entire scene was tranquil and homey.

Reuben leaned back against the grey barkless log, looked around and enjoyed and appreciated what he saw, this was what they both wanted and appreciated, time together in the wilderness of God's wonderful creation. The cicadas were beginning their ratcheting chorus that would soon provide the background for other sounds of the night. A distant cry of a lonesome coyote was lifted to the diminishing light, and a nighthawk soared overhead and sounded its cry as if calling for a mate. Reuben smiled, watching his woman busy and happy at her task, and looked forward to the night with the moon waxing full, his favorite time.

THEIR SECOND DAY ON THE TRAIL THEY FOLLOWED THE river called grand, but it was only impressive as to its meandering course, not its size, for in the valley it averaged just over fifty feet wide and seldom more than belly deep on the average horse. They continued almost due west, with the distant San Juan Mountains offering a jagged horizon. It was only as they approached the mouth of the canyon of the river that the foothills pushed in on them, breaking the monotonous terrain that was nothing more than a collection of sage, greasewood, rabbit brush, buffalo grass, and myriad cacti. Although it boasted ample coyotes and jackrabbits, the deer, elk, moose, and even the antelope did not get too far away from the fertile banks of the Rio Grande.

The nearby foothills were flanked with piñon, juniper, and cedar, but usually topped with rimrock and sided with talus slopes. A thin haze hung loosely in the distance, giving the further foothills and buttes a ghostly mirage appearance. The river was thick with cottonwoods, a few maple and boxelder, giving ample places for campsites and cover. Reuben and Elly found a site just before dusk and were busily making camp when Bear came to his feet, a low growl coming from deep within, and he tensed as he looked to the edge of the trees on the north side, his back to the campfire. Reuben came to his feet, rifle in hand as he went to a crouch, peering through the thickets to see beyond the trees. He heard the rattle of trace chains, the creak of wood, and squeal of wagon wheels, followed by the shouts of men.

He stood beside a big cottonwood, watching a big wagon drawn by a four-up of mules, creaking along a bit of a trail coming from the north. Several riders rode before and after the wagon. Reuben counted six men that he could see, could be more. Elly had come to his side, rifle in hand, and whispered, "What is it?"

"Looks like a company of gold seekers. They're not settlers, ain't no women among 'em, and no livestock other'n their horses," answered Reuben, also whispering.

"What're we gonna do?"

"Nuthin' right now," responded Reuben. He looked to the sky at the low light of dusk that was fading rapidly and back to the travelers. "We'll wait, see where they make camp, maybe I'll visit 'em then."

"You ain't leavin' me behind!" declared Elly.

"I won't. But you might just protect me from behind some cover. Don't know if they can be trusted right yet. They *are* in Indian country where they're not s'posed to be, so..."

"I FOUND IT! I FOUND IT!" SHOUTED PATRICK MATTHEWS as he ran and tumbled down the mountainside, waving his arms about, holding tight to a rolled up deerskin that held the parchment he had been guarding so carefully. "It's there, on the other side o' them rocks!" he shouted as he skidded to a stop beside the big wagon. He had hiked up the hill as he had done with several others that had been disappointing, but his broad smile told of his success. His enthusiasm was contagious and the other five men gathered around him and began peppering him with questions. "What's it look like?" "How big is it?" "Could you see anything else?" and more.

The group of men had joined together in South Park. They had all been some of the 'Johnny-come-lately' crowds that were too late for the gold claims and the wealth of gold being taken from around Fairplay, Buckskin, Tarryall, and more. With their disappointment being their common ground, they found each other in the Fairplay Hotel dining room and began sharing thoughts about what to do next. When Aiden McIntyre said, "It's like tryin' to find a buried treasure! Not knowin' nuthin' 'bout minin' gold, and all the claims taken, what're we gonna do?" he questioned, looking around the table at the others that were trying to drown their sorrows with the cheap whiskey.

A slow grin split the face of the one called Matthews as he leaned forward, looking around the table and at anyone nearby. He motioned to the others to draw close and began, "Funny you should say treasure. It just so happens I know about a treasure, south of here," he looked around conspiratorially, "and I ain't never told nobody about it till now. I used to be a muleskinner and a bullwhacker with a comp'ny that shipped goods to Santa Fe outta St. Louis. I met a feller in a pub in St. Louis who was pie-eyed drunk, and down in the mouth. We got to talkin', his name was LeBlanc and he had come upriver on the paddleboats, but he lost all his money to a card-sharp 'fore he got to town. Well, we got to talkin' and come to find out, he was a descendant of another LeBlanc I'd heard 'bout down in Santa Fe.

"Ya see, 'bout a hunnert years back, there was an expedition of Frenchies that were s'posed to map the French Territory, what we know of as Louisiana Territory." He looked from one to the other, making certain they were following his story, and continued. "Well, that expedition came through this country, well a bit south of here on the Rio Grande, and they was lookin' for gold and silver. They found 'em a bunch o' gold, rich stuff it were, an' sorta refined it and made 'em some bars an' such, but they got attacked by the Injuns. Most of 'em got kilt, but they was a small bunch lived, but couldn't carry the gold, cuz the Injuns took all their horses. So, they had to cache it. But they made 'em a map and took off back to N'awlins."

"N'awlins?" interrupted Sean McTavish, frowning.

"Yeah, you know, New Orleans, down in Louisiana," answered Matthews. He looked around, saw the eagerness in the eyes of the others, "So, by the time they got back to New Or'leans," he emphasized for McTavish, "there was only two of 'em left. One was a fella named LeBlanc. The other'n died within a couple days, and LeBlanc was the only one. He made a copy of the map, turned the first one o'er to the French authorities. But Leblanc wanted to go back to France, and he did. It was his young'uns that passed the map down and it was his grandson that I got it from."

The others leaned forward when Aiden McIntyre asked, "You have the map?"

Matthews grinned, nodding, "Ummhmm."

"Why didn't you go get it, the gold I mean?" asked McIntyre, frowning.

"I knew it'd take more'n just one. After all, there's Injuns in that country and one man couldn't do it by himself. I wanted to put together an expedition. That's why I came here, hopin' to at least make enough of a strike to fund a company of men to go look for the real stuff."

"How much gold is there s'posed to be?" asked the smaller man with the whiskery face known as Smitty. He was one of the many that went by the name of John Smith.

"I've heard about this treasure before, and I've heard numbers from five million to thirty million."

All the men looked from one to the other, smiles beginning to paint their faces and as they leaned back, they looked around the room to see if there was anyone nearby that might have heard. There was no one, the café was all but empty, save for the cook and waitress that were seated at a small table near the door to the kitchen, far enough away they could not have heard. The men looked at Matthews as George Leck asked, "So, would this bunch," motioning to the others at the table, "be enough?"

"I dunno, prob'ly. I don't know much about Injuns 'ceptin' they're better dead than alive," replied Matthews.

Leck looked around the table at the others, each man nodding his agreement, and he looked at Matthews. "Maybe we need to go someplace else where we can discuss this a little better," and rose from the table, motioning to the others to follow.

8 / QUEST

The six men were huddled together in the large oilcloth tent of Patrick Matthews. Attired much the same, trousers of canvas or wool, linen shirts, loose coats, wool hats, and high-topped leather work boots. The big Scottish cousins, Sean McTavish and Aiden McIntyre, were seated on the cot, Mickey Lemmon and George Leck sat on a pair of three-legged stools, while John 'Smitty' Smith sat on the ground looking up at Patrick Matthews as he began to tell more about the supposed treasure.

"Now, I've never been there, but I've talked to some who have. The headwaters of the Rio Grande are up in the San Juan Mountains, south of here about four- or five-days ride, maybe more. But there's plenty of trails, a few roads, but there's no tellin' what all till we get there."

"What about supplies?" asked Leck.

"From what I can find out, gettin' supplied would be best done here in Fairplay. There's nothin' 'tween here 'n there," answered Matthews.

"What'chu got and what do we need?"

"I've got a good wagon, a pair of mules, but we will

need another pair. It'd be best to have a four-up hitch." He motioned to the tent they were in, "I've got this tent, some supplies, a rocker box, some tools and pans, and my own personal gear."

The men looked around and began talking about their own gear and supplies. Mickey Lemmon held up his hands, looked at Matthews, "How's about we write this all down, then decide what we need and how we're gonna get it?" He looked around the group, "It sounds like everybody here is pitchin' in on this expedition, so we'll need to start a pot of funds so we can buy what we need."

"Good thinkin'," answered Matthews. He looked back at Lemmon, "Can you write?" and when Lemmon nodded, he added, "Then start writin'!"

As the men began sharing ideas and plans, the two Scottish cousins leaned close as Aiden looked at Sean, "What are you thinkin' about all this?"

Sean chuckled, "Look cousin, we came out here together, knowing very little about gold finding, and the way I think is that one place is as good as another. Even if this *treasure* has little truth to it, it's as much as we knew about this place. So, while he's lookin' for treasure, we can be lookin' for gold!"

Aiden grinned, "That's 'bout what I was thinkin' too. Even if there's no treasure, where we're goin' there apparently was gold at one time to hatch such a story as this, so even if it's got a wee bit o' truth to it, it's as good as anything else we've followed!"

"Aye," chuckled Sean, turning his attention back to the others.

The next few hours were spent compiling a list of needed supplies, subtracting those that each man had on hand, and adding additional items, such as rifles and ammunition, that might be of more use in Indian territory. When they finished the list, the duties were portioned out with the Scotsmen taking the task of finding the four-up hitch and the two extra mules and other gear that would be best found at the blacksmith. Lemmon and Leck were tasked with getting the rifles and ammunition, while Matthews and Smitty went to the Emporium for the needed supplies.

They were on the trail south by midday, using the noon meal as their good-bye to South Park. The blacksmith had told of a southern route often taken by those going to California Gulch or Oro City, that would take them over the mountains and to the Arkansas River Valley. "And I heerd tell of a trail that'd take ya oe'r the upper end o' the Sangres. Seems there's a crick that comes from the southwest and meets the south fork o' the Arkansas. It's up that crick the trail takes ya' into the San Looey Valley," he explained between spitting his tobacco through his whiskery filter and banging the big hammer on the hot steel to fashion some tool. He looked up at the two big Scotsmen, squinted a mite and wiped the tobacco juice from his chin whiskers with his ragged sleeves of his union suit, chuckled, "Don't know why you'd wanna go there, that's the land o' them Utes, Apache, and Navvyjoes! Good way ta' lose yore hair!"

———

IT WAS NEARING MIDDAY ON THE SEVENTH DAY OUT OF Fairplay when Patrick Matthews came vaulting down the rocky slope of the rimrock-topped butte shouting, "I found it! I found it!" When the others had gathered around, he excitedly pointed at the unrolled parchment. "See here!" he was pointing to a small sketch of a rock formation with a big hole. "This is the natural rock arch *La Ventana,* the Window!" He looked at the others, saw nothing but frowns, and continued, "See here. This is the first landmark. From here we go south to the big river, go upstream," as he spoke, he moved his finger along the lines of the map, "to the south fork of that river. Then it's," he looked at the map, touching the points of intersecting lines, "the third creek from the south. Then this long high ridge, and just beyond...*there!*" pointing to an *X* that marked the location of the treasure.

The others leaned forward, looking at the map, excitement and enthusiasm spreading like a flame, splitting faces with grins and each one nodding. Mumbles, exclamations of agreement, and more came from the men until the Scotsmen said together, "Then let's get ta' movin'!"

The detour to the first landmark demanded by Matthews had taken them about five miles from the main trail or rough wagon road on the west edge of the valley, now they had to backtrack to resume their southward journey. When they turned up the wide arroyo, most of the men grumbled and complained, but grudgingly continued. Now, with the first landmark discovered, they were filled with excitement and wild imaginations of vast riches and there was no grumbling or complaining and faces were painted with smiles.

Keeping the rugged and juniper-covered foothills off their right shoulders, the small caravan had topped a slight rise and now had an easygoing, slightly downhill grade, and according to the map, should soon see sign of the Rio Bravo del Norte. Smitty had taken point and he shouted back to the others, waited for them to catch up and excitedly pointed to the long line of green that hopefully showed the long river they had been seeking.

The irregular shoulders of the foothills crowded closer and in the distance to the south, taller mountains showed with their heads in the clouds and what appeared to be a spring storm letting loose its load of water on the contours of the mountain range. George Leck had joined Smitty on the point and the two men rode side by side, most often quiet as the men that came from the flatlands of farm country the near side of the Mississippi, gazed at the distant mountains and listened to the low thunder of the faraway storm. "Sure is different country out here, ain't it?" asked Leck, glancing to his riding partner.

"It be that, fer sure'n certain!" answered Smitty. He twisted around in his saddle, looking at the wagon and others that followed, "They be ketchin' up, guess we oughta pick up the pace, see if we can find us a campsite fer t'night." He squeezed his legs against his bay gelding, taking him up to a trot and then a canter. Leck followed close behind and soon came alongside. The men rocked to the quickened pace of the horses, chuckling to themselves as they watched long-eared jackrabbits hightailing it out of the way. They kept up the pace for most of a mile, then dropped back to a good walk, the horses blowing and bobbing their heads. Smitty said, "That'll wake a feller up, now, won't it?"

"Sure 'nuff!" answered Leck. He nodded in the distance, "Looks like the trail bends around that point, maybe goes up a canyon where the river comes from. Might be a good place to camp." He looked up at the fading light, the sun already dropping behind the hills on their right, "And dark's comin'!"

"Let's point 'em to them bigger cottonwoods yonder, by the river. That oughta be good." Smitty pointed to the thickets of the tall trees, leaves blowing in the light wind, with undergrowth of brush broken to give an inviting break. They pushed into the greenery, looked around at what appeared to be a previously used campsite that also offered grass for animals and enough space for the wagon and more. The whiskery man looked at Leck, "You wanna go bring the wagon in, or you want me to do it?"

"You go ahead on, I'll start gatherin' some firewood and such. They're not too far back and I'll have a fire goin' 'fore they get'chere."

FROM THE TREES NO MORE THAN TWO HUNDRED YARDS downstream, Reuben and Elly watched as the wagon and men moved into the trees to make their camp for the night. Reuben looked at Elly, "I'm not too sure 'bout those fellas, they don't appear to be outlaws, more like prospectors with the wagon and such. Maybe we'll just watch from afar, trail 'em a ways, listen in on 'em." He glanced at his woman, saw her nod her agreement, and looked back at the riders as they followed the wagon into the trees.

Reuben stood tall, lowered his rifle and taking a deep breath that lifted his shoulders, he shook his head and said, "I dunno. I'm gettin' that bad feelin' that something's not right. You know, when your skin seems to crawl, goes right up your spine, and makes your stomach turn over?"

Elly grinned, nodding, "Ummhmm, but as often as not, it's just you gettin' hungry!"

Reuben chuckled, slipped his arm around her waist and said, "Well then, maybe you better get busy fixin' our supper! I'm gonna shinny up that knob behind our camp and see if I can see anythin' 'fore it gets too dark!"

"Ummhmm, why am I not surprised? Every time there's work to do, you skedaddle off and climb some mountain, just for the fun of it and have yourself a look-see, even when you can't see!" She shook her head, giggled a little, and watched as he grabbed his binoculars and trotted from the trees to take to the pointed knob that rose about a hundred feet higher than their camp.

9 / STRANGERS

Even though the light was fading, it was easy to see the camp of the men. Their fire was larger than necessary, giving warmth, light, and heat for cooking but also providing a brilliant beacon for any interested passersby like the many Ute and Apache that inhabited the area. The smoke could be seen as long as there was light and could be smelled by anyone within a couple miles. Reuben shook his head at the ignorance of the greenhorns that undoubtedly thought only of their comfort rather than awareness of their surroundings and danger. But he also knew there were many that felt the fire provided safety from the wild animals, like bears, wolves, and coyotes, and he knew they were getting into bear country. He grinned at the thought of these newcomers coming face-to-face with the big grizzly.

Reuben lifted his binoculars to look at the group, saw the six men gathered near the fire, the horses and mules picketed near the water, and few firearms within reach of anyone. He watched them a moment longer, then scanned the area for any sign of others, but seeing none, he rose from his promontory and started his return. He moved as quiet as the wind and slipped back into camp. The site was on the south bank of the river, while the others had their camp on the north bank and further upstream, well out of sight. Reuben dropped to the flat rock near the fire, looked at Elly, "I think I'll need to get close, listen a mite, get a better idea what they're up to, 'fore we go introducin' ourselves. If they live long enough, that is." He shook his head as he accepted the plate of hot food from Elly, "They are sure enough greenhorns. They've got a fire big enough to send a message all the way back to Fort Garland that they're here!" He grinned at his woman, smiled, "Thank you, darlin'."

"You're welcome, but how 'bout you givin' thanks to the Lord for His blessings?"

"I can do that," he answered and dropped his head as he began to say a prayer of thanksgiving for their many blessings and for a wonderful wife that was such a good cook. He chuckled as he said "Amen" and smiled up at his grinning wife who playfully punched him on his shoulder. She sat beside him, her own full plate on her lap and began eating, using the fresh biscuit as a 'pusher' to get all the stew on the big spoon.

"Well, if you're just gonna be listenin', I s'pose I could let you go by yourself, but it'd be better if you had comp'ny," she declared, looking at her man as he sipped his hot coffee.

"I reckon," he shrugged, and finished his food, setting the tin plate aside. "It'll take us a little while to sneak up on 'em, there's plenty of cover, but with six of 'em listenin' it might get a mite touchy."

"Any of 'em look like they know their way around the woods?" asked Elly.

"No...well, maybe one, he's the littlest but he's also a mite older and has whiskers like a mountain man."

"Mountain men ain't the only ones that grow whiskers," declared Elly, frowning at her man.

"Yeah, but..." replied Reuben, and shrugged again.

Dusk had dropped the curtain on daylight and the stars were lighting their lanterns when Reuben and Elly started from their camp, Bear at their side, to work their way through the trees and across the river. As Reuben slipped into the water, the cold shocked him and he gritted his teeth, stopping in place and looking back at Elly, "You sure you wanna do this – it's cold!"

"Oh, you sissy," she said as she stepped into the water and quickly hugged him for some warmth. "Ooooh, it *is* cold!"

"Sissy?" he said, as he pulled her close as they moved together through the water. Bear had plunged in and easily paddled his way to the far shore, shook off the excess, and stood on the bank, waiting for the two.

They wiped the water from their buckskins and quickly stepped into the thicker trees, using the matted and damp leaves to muffle any sounds they might make as they moved. The fire still blazed, lighting the entire clearing, and painting the trees with a golden hue, casting skeletal shadows into the depths of the woods. The men were a mite rowdy and boisterous as Reuben and Elly neared. The two stayed in the deeper shadows and darkness, but carefully stole as close as they felt was safe, and with the men doing little to stifle their talk, it was easy to hear their noisy conversations.

"Best idee you had since we started, Patrick! It's good to celebrate once in a while, ain't it boys?" declared the whiskery older man.

"Aye laddie, it is good to wet our whistle now and

again!" said one of the two big men, both with the typical Scottish look about their big frames, red hair, whiskers, and flashing eyes.

"So, how long ya think it'll take?" asked a somber figure as he lifted the mason jug with his crooked elbow.

"How long, what?" answered Patrick.

"To get where we're goin'!" added the somber man, bringing the jug to his lips and taking a deep draught.

"Dunno. Depends on how far them cricks are and if we find the clues," answered Patrick, accepting the jug from the drinker.

"Well, we ain't in no hurry," said the man that sat off by himself, refusing to take the jug. "I figger on doin' a little pannin' along the way, see if we can find any color."

"What're we gonna do if we see any Injuns?" asked the other Scotsman, accepting the jug from Patrick and beginning to lift it for a drink.

"Kill 'em! It's the only way! If this is Injun country like they say, an' if any of 'em see us, they'd just go tell others, so it's best just to kill 'em as we sees 'em!" answered Patrick, beginning to slur his words as he belched.

"We brought some trade goods, wouldn't it be better to try to talk, make a little trade, see if they know anything about where we can find gold? I mean, what's it gonna hurt, we can always kill 'em later, can't we?" asked the Scotsman.

"Mebbe, but not good to take chances. I'm kinda partial to my hair an' don't wanna have no Injun takin' it from me," slurred Patrick, sliding off the log and dropping on his haunches beside it, his chin dropping to his chest as he sat immobile, eyes closed, looking as if he had fallen asleep.

The bigger Scotsman looked at Patrick, chuckled, and lifted the jug for another drink. He lowered it and handed it to his cousin, and both men chuckled at the passed-out Patrick, saw Leck slowly lean to the side and drop to his stomach, also out for the night. "Aye, and these lil' ones canna hol' their liquor!"

"Not like a good Scotsman!" answered his cousin, lifting the jug to drain it dry.

Reuben looked at Elly, nodded to the darkness and started away from the camp of the men. Within a few moments they were back in their own camp as Reuben put a few small, dry sticks on the coals of their fire to get some warmth and to dry off their duds. He stood beside it, turned his back to it, and looked at Elly, her somber expression showing her fear for the men and what they said about the natives. "They're just like so many others, they believe what a few say and other stupid things they hear and assume all natives want to kill and scalp all white men. It's just not right!" she declared, stomping her foot to show her contempt for such stupidity.

"There's always gonna be those that listen to others and never try to find out the truth of the matter. We've been fortunate to get acquainted with so many native peoples and know there are good and bad among all tribes, red and white. But we've never assumed anything about any of them, except maybe the Comanche," he spat as he remembered his first fight with the Comanche.

Elly shook her head, "You know I have no love for those that took us captive, but you know as well as I do that there are even some Comanche that are good people."

"Yeah, I know. But we're in Ute and Apache country, and from what the captain said, just south of here is Navajo country. But maybe if we get ahead of them," suggested Reuben, nodding toward the camp of the prospectors, "we can get to Kaniache and keep them from gettin' in a fight with these greenhorns."

"Maybe. It's worth a try. Especially since Ouray and the Tabeguache are willing to make peace, maybe we can convince Kaniache to do the same," answered Elly, hopefully and letting a slow smile paint her face at the thought of peace with the Ute.

"Then we better get a little sleep 'fore we head out. We'll have to get a mighty early start to get past 'em 'fore first light," resolved Reuben, starting toward their blankets.

10 / SAN JUANS

The lazy moon peeked out over the edge of the dark clouds, giving just enough light for Reuben and Elly to work through the trees as they made their way along the edge of the cottonwoods that stood thick on the south bank of the big river. A narrow, grassy flat stretched between the knoll that had been Reuben's promontory lookout just hours before, but now stood as a lone sentinel to mark the wide mouth of the valley that carried Pinos Creek to its confluence with the Rio Bravo del Norte. They rounded the shoulder of the knoll and pointed their horses into the shadowy draw that came from the south. This lower end of the valley carried both the Pinos and the east branch of the Pinos. Further into the valley, the creek split and stretched across the grassy flat, only to meet the bigger river before the mouth of the main canyon.

The valley was wide with low shoulders of the foothills pushing back from the fertile flats that had been host to many native encampments over the years and many seasons past. As they rode, Reuben took note of the vegetation, tall grasses dancing in the moonlight, round-shouldered rabbitbrush, and scattered shade offering inviting cover for rabbits, sage hens, ground squirrels and even coyotes, badgers, and more. The moon had freed itself of the dark clouds and now painted the landscape in muted blues and greys as the silent hours of early morning welcomed the two riders.

Reuben nodded to the flats, "There haven't been any villages in this valley in a couple years, that grass is tall and untouched."

"This *is* one of the areas the captain spoke about that the Mouache Ute used for their encampments, isn't it?" asked Elly, looking 'round about in the dim light.

"Ummhmm, but if it was used before, it hasn't been used in at least two seasons, maybe more. Maybe they camped further up, might find 'em come daylight," suggested Reuben.

"Or they're in a totally different valley. It's not like they don't have a few to choose from."

Reuben chuckled, "You're right about that."

"Do you really think we'll find them? Kaniache and the Ute, I mean."

"Hope so, but if not, we'll look in some of the other valleys. At the least, we'll get to know the area and maybe see what the prospectors and others are doing to upset the captain so," answered Reuben, looking at the eastern hills to judge the approach of the morning sun.

Higher hills cloaked in black timber and night shadows stood before them, the taller ones on the east edge that would catch the first light of early morning. Off their right shoulder, thick juniper and cedar appeared as big-chested soldiers of the dark, lone watchmen protecting the western hills. It required little imagination to see them march alongside to escort the visitors deeper into the narrowing valley.

The valley was wide and fertile at its mouth, stretching about two miles across, but the further they moved into the mountains, it narrowed. As they approached a dog-leg bend to the west, the valley was about two hundred yards wide and narrowing as they moved further south and higher into the mountains. By late morning, it was little more than an arroyo, the hills rose higher, and they approached a fork in the creek. This area was much the same as the rest of the mountain valleys and the ridges that lined them. North-facing slopes were black with thick timber, spruce, fir, pines and more, while the south-facing slopes were semi-bald with scattered juniper and piñon. The canyon bottom showed green due to the runoff-carrying creeks that kept the willows, alders, and berry bushes plentiful. They stopped at the confluence of the two branches of the creek, found shade at the point of the ridge that separated the two forks, and after loosening the girths on the animals, they let them water and graze during the short rest. Reuben and Elly sat side by side in the shade of a tall ponderosa as they watched the horses and admired the hillsides and canyon. With some pemmican in hand, they watched the hat-sized fire lick the bottom of the coffee pot readying the hot brew for their brief respite.

Elly closed her eyes and breathed deeply, stretched her arms wide and said, "Ummm there's nothing as sweet as a cool morning and the smell of pines in the clear mountain air."

Reuben smiled as he leaned on one elbow, legs stretched out before him, and looked at his woman, always proud of her and happy with her as he mumbled his agreement to her expression, "Ummhmmm, just like back at our cabin."

"Yes, it is, but that doesn't make it any less enjoyable!" she declared.

Reuben frowned, sat up, sniffing the air and frowned at Elly, "Smell that?"

"What is it?" asked Elly, looking at her man and frowning at the new odor.

"Elk, lots of 'em. Back that way," he pointed past the point of the ridge, "Prob'ly comin' down that fork." He stood and walked to the horses, picking up their reins and the mule's lead and drawing them back to the tree line. Elly made a low whistle to call Bear near, slapping her leg to get his attention and bringing him close.

A low rumble told of many hooves, some clattering against rocks. Other sounds, the mew and glug of moving elk, mostly cows, and the squeal and bleat of new calves. The multi-colored animals began to parade along the east fork of the little creek, some clattering through the creek bottom and pushing through the willows, all on the move. The crooked necks in dark brown, long legs and bellies of the same color, sides and back of dusty tan, and rumps of faded yellow/white, the big animals crashed through the brush and made their way into the lower valley. If there were any bulls, they were young ones and had yet to show growths of antlers. Playful calves, looking more orange than their mothers, gamboled about, kicking up heels and running around, oblivious to any danger.

The parade lasted several minutes, and Reuben guessed there to be at least two hundred plus of the stunning animals. He looked at Elly who stood, hands clasped as she held them to her mouth, eyes sparkling with wonder, hardly able to stand still as if she wanted to run and jump with the herd. Reuben chuckled, shook his head, and said, "Magnificent, aren't they?"

"Ohhh yes! Beautiful!" she declared, watching the last of the herd chase after the others.

As they watched, their attention was turned as Bear growled, dropping his head between his shoulder, looking through the point of trees to the far timber covered slope. Grey shadows flitted through the trees, and Reuben muttered, "Wolves!"

Elly turned to look at her man and back to the trees. She saw the swift-moving creatures, several with tongues lolling, all moving together, grey, black, dusty brown, a big black in the lead. It was a large pack, and Elly quickly counted as they flitted through the trees, "There's more'n twenty, maybe thirty of them! That's a big pack!"

She looked at Reuben, fear on her face, "They can't take on that herd, can they?"

He shook his head, "No, they'll just go for stragglers, calves, any animal they can catch off by themselves. But the herd'll fight for each other, although I'm sure the wolves will get some."

"Oh, that's terrible!" she declared, looking down canyon after the herd. "Those poor babies!"

"Why? The wolves have to eat too!" he declared, shaking his head.

"Well, yeah, but..." she looked down the canyon again, fearful of seeing a carnage, but the herd had passed the bend and were out of sight.

"They've made the wider valley, it'll be better for the calves, more room to run," said Reuben, making an effort to console his worried woman.

"Good, but let's move out. If there's anything else followin' that herd, I don't want to see it!" she declared, reaching for the rein of her appaloosa.

It was a well-used game trail that kept to the north-facing slope in the thick timber and offered ample cover for the two travelers. Continually moving southwest, the trail steadily climbed into the higher reaches of the mountains. The hillside flanked the long ridge that stretched from the granite-tipped peaks that still held snow in the crevices and crevasses, and the air was cool as they climbed ever higher. By mid-afternoon, the timbered shoulders pushed back from the creek bottom and formed a wide basin, thick with lodgepole pine and tall, slender fir, but standing regally above the basin was a long ridge stretching north to south, a thin line of snow cornices hanging at the top edge to show itself as the spine of the big granite-topped rim. Scarred by avalanche and rockslide paths and jagged shoulders and finger ridges, the long granite formation appeared as the grave of a giant, the flanks flaring out in broad shoulders that showed sign of a missing village. Tipi rings marked the central compound of the once large village, but they had been overgrown with new spring growth grasses. This must have been the village of the Ute for the previous year, but it was an encouraging sign for the two searchers.

They both had spotted and recognized the sign of the village and looked at one another. Elly spoke first, "What a beautiful location! The mountain behind them, the vast basin that must have been rich with game, lots of grass for their animals, and look at that scenery!" she nodded down the long valley that spread like open arms before them.

"Yeah, but we wanted to find the village where they are now!" declared Reuben.

"But they wouldn't be this high unless they just moved to some place like this. They couldn't spend a winter there, why, it must be chin deep in snow through the winter!"

"Yeah, but if they were here last summer, they won't be coming here this summer." He paused, looking at the sight, and turned to look and the high mountain range south of them at the headwaters of the creek they had followed. "Maybe if we get a little higher, we can see more country and spot 'em in their new camp."

Elly chuckled, "You're just like so many other men, always wanting to see what's 'over the next mountain!"

"You do too, admit it!" answered Reuben, reining the big blue roan back to the trail, nodding to the high mountains, "We've got a ways to go before we sleep! And I'm not likin' the looks of those clouds yonder," nodding to the south at the boiling dark clouds.

11 / HIGH COUNTRY

They topped out to a boggy basin that lay between the granite-tipped peaks. Skirting the timberline of the high country, the trail took the west edge of the basin, hugging the few trees, mountain mahogany, bristlecone pine, and a few struggling aspen. Reuben twisted around in his saddle, pointing to the trail ahead, "Looks to be a bit of a saddle there. Maybe we can make it over to the other side, find some shelter to spend the night."

The trail was buried under a deep snowdrift. They nudged the horses to the high side, edging the trees on their left, overlooking the drift on their right, letting the horses pick their own way on the uncertain terrain. As they rounded a point of rocks, they were in a hanging basin. Long glacier drifts lay before them, steep rocky talus to their left, allowing the only way through was to take to the tundra and hope to cross a strip of glacier to make it to the barren, rocky top of the peak. Reuben stopped, looking at the possibilities. He looked at Elly, pointed at the game trail before them, "If we take that'n, we'll hafta cross that strip of glacier, and after that is the longer part up further." He turned to his right, pointing to the steeper slope on the west, "If we take that'n, it's a steeper climb at first and more snow, and from here I can't tell how deep it might be..." He looked back at the first trail then to Elly. "What'chu think?"

She nodded to the first choice, "That one looks better to me. This one," pointing to their right, "looks a lot deeper and steeper. I don't wanna try that'n."

"Then this is the one," declared Reuben, nudging Blue forward. They were high, past timberline and probably nearing 12,000 feet. The air was thin and cold, steam came from the horses' nostrils, lather was showing under the martingale and saddle pads. They had to find shelter soon and rub down the horses. Tiny blue forget-me-not blossoms lined the trailside, and some even smaller moss campion bloomed purple. A fat yellow-bellied marmot sat up, staring at the strange visitors, watching them push their horses toward the glacier. A glance to the ridge above them showed a bighorn sheep showing his white belly as he stood tall, staring down the rocky talus and the invaders to his domain.

Reuben and Elly had hunkered down in their winter coats, Elly with her wolfskin coat and Reuben in his wool capote. Both had scarves around their necks and hats pulled low as they faced the cold air whipping over the crest of the bald, granite saddle. As they approached the drift, Blue paused, dropping his head to look at the snow and carefully putting his hoof on the edge. As Reuben dug heels into his ribs, the big roan stepped out, digging in his hooves, and lunging ahead. The crust gave way slightly, allowing the hooves to dig into the melting, slushy layer, gaining traction as the big horse lunged forward, fighting for every foothold and Reuben clasping his sides with his long legs, feet burrowing deep in the stirrups. With a loose rein, the roan kept his eyes on the soil less than thirty yards away and he scrambled, slipping, and sliding but digging all the way until his front hooves caught traction on the dirt and pulled himself free of the icy glacier. Once on good footing, Reuben stopped the roan, stepped down and looked back at Elly. "Give the mule his lead, slap him on the butt and let him come!" he hollered, pointing to the pack mule who had stood staring as his blue roan friend fought the ice.

Elly pulled the lead, bringing the mule alongside, threw the lead over his neck and slapped his rump to get him started. The sure-footed beast carefully picked his first step, then leaned into the steep snowbank and dug in, moving with his amazing agility, and simply walked up the steeper icy slope, and stepped off to move beside Blue. Reuben chuckled, shook his head, and hollered to Elly, "If you want to try it, come ahead on, but if you want to walk it and lead the mare, you can give that a shot."

She pushed the appaloosa closer to the edge of the snow, showing the churned snow and ice from the other animals, and with a glance to Reuben, she slapped legs to the mare and started up the glacier. The trail was easier for the mare, with the crust broken, the snow dug by the others. The mare readily to quickly make her crossing and stopped on the dryer tundra. Elly leaned forward, elbow on the pommel, and smiled at Reuben who stood beside his roan. "Nothin' to it!" she giggled.

"Then you lead the way up and over the top, but watch yourself, that wind is cold enough to freeze the end of your nose off!" chuckled Reuben, stepping into the stirrup and swinging aboard his mount.

Elly kept to the edge of the bigger glacier, staying on

the dry ground that was covered with low-growing plants of the tundra, the rocks sporting orange and grey lichen. She leaned low on the neck of the mare, reaching down to stroke her neck and encourage the little horse as she picked her way up the steeper slope. As they neared the crest, the wind howled over the saddle, reminding her of her Irish heritage and a grandfather that spoke of the women of the fairy mound called banshees. He would tell of the horrendous screams that would haunt the darkest nights, and how parents would use those sounds to scold misbehaving children, warning them the banshees were coming for bad little boys and girls.

As they dropped over the crest, Reuben pointed and shouted to be heard above the howling winds, "There!" pointing to the black of trees a little over a mile across the rolling slope of the south-facing mountain. He motioned for her to follow and nudged the big roan to ride the slight rise that would keep them from the uncertain boggy ground that marked the snowmelt of recent days and often held uncertain footing. They pushed across the narrow basin, moved into the trees to escape the wind, and reined up to look around. "This looks good for now. We've enough light left to make camp, maybe put together a bit of a shelter, at least for tonight."

Elly nodded, slipped off the mare, dropping the rein to ground tie her and looked at Reuben, "You take care of the animals, I'll get us a fire going. I'm freezing!" she said, slapping her hands together and lifting her shoulders.

"Alright, go ahead. I'll take care of 'em. There's water in the bottom yonder. I'll strip 'em, rub 'em down, take 'em to water and fill the coffee pot while I'm at it." There was scattered elk sedge and pine grass among the trees and near the little creek, enough for the animals to get some graze. Reuben picketed them within reach of both graze and water, but with a look to the sky, knew he would need to bring them back into the trees if the storm hit.

As Elly puttered about the fire, broiling some strips of meat and warming some leftover cornmeal biscuits, Reuben busied himself making a lean-to between two tall fir trees, using the lower branches to make the cover and a sapling for the cross bar. He knew it would not be watertight, but it would help. He stood back to look at his handiwork and consoled himself with, "Better'n nothin'!" He shook his head as he added, mumbling, "Just hope it ain't too bad a storm!"

Elly heard and understood, "Me too! But the way it's been blowin' it might be lettin' up or movin' on past."

Reuben looked skyward, the light dimming with the setting sun and fading dusk, but the few clouds overhead promised neither storm nor clear and he shook his head, knowing the high-country storms could be merciless, but also might be nothing but winds and noise. He was hopeful for the latter. Bear lay at Reuben's feet, showing no sign of stress or strain, lifting only one eyebrow to look at the two, and close them again, not interested in anything they were doing.

"NUTHIN'!" SPAT GEORGE LECK, LOOKING UP AT SMITTY. The whiskery man sat in his saddle, leaning his elbow on the pommel, and holding the reins in his hand as he looked at the exasperated man kneeling on the bank of the little creek. With a gold pan in his hand, Leck stretched, looking up and down the creek, nodded toward a big boulder in the middle of the trickling water, "I'm gonna try a pan there, below that big boulder!" He struggled to his feet, waded into the creek, and kicked around the bottom with his boots, bent over and scooped up some sand and rock and started swirling the water around, glaring into the shallow pan and searching for anything that might be a flake of gold. He shook his head, looked back at Smitty, "Nuthin'!"

Smitty chuckled, "Didja expect to find the mother lode with yore first pan?"

Leck started wading back to the shore and stepped onto the grassy bank beside the man, "No, but it'd be nice if we did!" he declared. "One thing for sure, that water's plumb cold, I mean to tell ya! I prob'ly won't feel my toes till suppertime!" he grumbled, stomping his feet to try to get some blood circulating.

"I'm goin' on ahead, do some scoutin', there's another crick just around that point yonder," declared Smitty, nodding toward the end of the ridge that pushed the river into a wide bend, "and 'nother'n across the way. If'n you git tarred o' pannin', switch off with one o' them Scotsmen. They's big 'nuff to walk across the river an' not get more'n their boots wet!"

Leck looked at the whiskery scout, "We gonna try ever' crick?"

"Course we are! Unless you know which'ns got gold and which'ns don't!" chuckled the older man, slapping legs to his mount to resume his scout further upstream of the big river. He had no sooner rounded the point than the wagon came in sight on the trail that rode the shoulder of the foothills to the north of the river. Leck fetched his mount, swung aboard, and waited for the wagon to draw near. Driven by Patrick Matthews, the wagon slowed and Matthews looked at Leck, "Been pannin' already have you?" asked Patrick.

"Yup, but no color yet. Gonna try that next crick, maybe cross o'er to that'n yonder," pointing to the creek that came from the south and entered the big river just above the point of land behind him.

"The others are on the far side. They tried two or three creeks over there, no luck. But there's plenty more. Who knows, we might strike it big and not hafta find the treasure!" suggested Patrick, shrugging.

"Hah! Even if we hit it, I'm still follerin' that map there. Cain't never have too much gold for my thinkin'!" replied Leck, nudging his horse ahead of the wagon to get to the creek around the point.

It was their first full day of traveling beside the Rio Bravo del Norte. The sky was clear and blue when they began, but as the day wore on more clouds rolled in and the wind kicked up, causing the flatlanders to look around at the surrounding hills and mountains and begin to wonder just what kind of storm they may be driving into, but the lure of riches dimmed their judgment. They pushed on until the mules were showing tired and the men had been discouraged by the lack of color in the many streams. Patrick Matthews had driven the wagon all day and he decided it was time to make camp. They approached the confluence of the river and the south fork that came from a long valley that pointed southward. He pulled up to the bank just above the confluence, stepped down, and looked at the flow of the river. Just above the confluence, between two bends in the river, the water trickled over a gravelly bottom, showing the water to be rather shallow and looking to be an easy crossing. As he stepped back aboard the wagon, the three men that had been trying the south side streams showed themselves as they came from the thickets on the far side, Sean McTavish cupped his hands and hollered, "Looks to be a good crossin'! Come on across, we'll wait for ye!"

Matthews waved his response and slapped reins to the mules, shouting, "Heeyup mules!" and urged them into the water. It proved to be an easy crossing and the men pointed Patrick to the thickets of cottonwoods on the peninsula between the rivers for their campsite. He had just pulled the wagon to a stop when the other two men, Smitty and Leck, followed the wagon to cross the river and reined up beside the others. Mickey Lemmon had been rather quiet, but spoke up before the others, "I'm goin' upstream a ways, see if I can find some fresh meat. Smitty, how 'bout you comin' along?"

Smitty nodded, glanced to the others, and nudged his mount to follow Mickey. The others quickly set to and began their tasks of establishing their camp as Patrick suggested, "We might wanna pull the wagon o'er yonder, use it for the shelter." He looked to the sky, "Might come a storm tonight!"

12 / STALK

The wind howled and screamed through the trees and whipped over the crests of the bald mountains that dared to lift their hoary heads into the black sky of night. The clouds were heavy and snuffed out the lanterns of the stars, leaving nothing but blackness in their wake. Treetops swayed and bent to the will of the wind, horses stomped and pushed together, sharing their warmth. The pine bough covering of the shelter ruffled under the tarp that whipped and snapped its protests. Reuben and Elly snuggled close, pulling the blankets over their shoulders and Bear pushed against the back of Elly, sharing, and receiving warmth.

The storm proved to be nothing more than dark clouds flexing their muscles and huffing and puffing their bravado against those that would dare to enter the domain of uninhabited wilderness. As the grey light of early morning shook its blanket across the canopy and bid the darkness adieu, Reuben rolled from his blankets and stood to stretch beside the ruffled lean-to, smiling at his woman who showed only the top of her head as she crawled deeper into the warm wool blankets. He grabbed up his Sharps, his binoculars, Bible, and possibles pouch and started up the slope behind their camp.

As he crested the knob behind the camp, he did his first look-around and chose a spot on the bald ridge and sat on the mat of tundra, crossing his legs, and reaching for his Bible. He heard a faint scream and looked up to see the widespread wings of a bald eagle bidding his good morning. A glance to a higher peak showed white that moved and Reuben grinned as he recognized the agility of a mountain goat, leading the way down the high peak with a little kid behind. He dropped his eyes and caught the movement of a yellow-bellied marmot, early from his den to greet the new morning. Reuben smiled and opened the Scriptures to Psalm 50 and began reading at verse 10. The words seemed to whisper to him, *For every beast of the forest is mine, and the cattle upon a thousand hills. I know all the fowls of the mountains: and the wild beasts of the field are mine.*

Reuben lifted his eyes to enjoy the wonder of God's creation as the first light of morning began to push shadows into the crevices and ravines, lengthen the shadows of the forests, and magnify the sounds of the high country. He smiled and lifted his shoulders as he breathed deep and began to pray and offer his thanksgiving to the Almighty God. He whispered the *Amen* and reached for his binoculars. He wanted to find some sign of the Mouache Ute camp, some indication where to go to look and hopefully meet with Kaniache and talk peace with the great leader of the Ute people. He knew their summer encampment would be in the high country, but they would favor wide mountain meadows plentiful with graze and game.

The mountains to the south and the far north were the pillars of the sky, standing tall and proud with nothing between the granite summits and the blue of the sky where they appeared to scratch the azure dome with their needle-tipped peaks. Reuben and Elly had come from the east and the shoulders of the mountains to the west seemed to cradle long, deep valleys thick with black timber yet beckoning with long snakes of green that twisted through the bottoms.

As he scanned the country, he saw a few elk, a couple bighorn sheep, timberline bucks, and the many scars on the mountainside that told of long-ago avalanches and rockslides where limestone slide-rock, covered with lichen, teetered upon one another as they clung to the steep mountain sides. Rocky escarpments jutted from trees to tell of broad shoulders that refused to fall, and talus slopes that were the last remains of other outcroppings that time wore away. Yet wherever he looked, he saw no smoke, no tipi poles standing above the pines, no horse herds watched over by young warriors, no fresh sign of any native village.

He leaned back on his elbows, the binoculars resting on his chest as he looked about, enjoying the peaceful early morning. A scan of the sky told of distant clouds that might form into storm clouds, but for now the day promised sunshine and blue sky. He came to his feet, stretched, and started back to camp, hopeful of smelling coffee brewing and maybe some pork belly frying.

"See anything?" asked Elly as she saw her man coming through the trees. She stood, hands on hips, watching him return.

"Just a lot of beautiful country, some animals, but no sign of a village. But one thing for sure, there's about a couple hundred places out there where a village could be, and we'd never find it unless we stumbled into it!" grumbled Reuben as he looked at the coffee pot dancing on the rock beside the little fire. He smiled up at Elly, bent for a cup and reached for the pot but stooped lower to pick up a mitten to grab it with, and poured himself a steaming, hot cup of java. He looked at Elly with a question on his face and she nodded, so he handed her that cup and poured another for himself.

They sat beside one another on the broad, flat boulder that was near the fire and they blew on the coffee before cautiously taking the first sip. Elly broke the silence, "So, now what?"

Reuben lowered his cup, looked at his woman with a broad smile and said, "We keep goin'. If nothin' else, we'll see some beautiful country, and maybe learn our way around a mite. If we don't find Kaniache's band, maybe they'll find us," he shrugged, lifting the cup for a little more. "Maybe after breakfast we'll head west. There's a long, wide valley that way, and another'n cross the ridge to the north of that'n. Either one of 'em could be a good summer encampment for the Mouache."

"We'll need to get some fresh meat too," suggested Elly, looking at the last of their meat sizzling over the flames.

"We can do that," answered Reuben, putting his arm around Elly and drawing her close.

Bear led the way as they started to the west, pointing to the start of the long canyon that Reuben had spied out on his early morning look-see. There was a bit of a creek that worked its way around an opposing pair of ridge points and a good game trail, probably used for decades and more, sided the creek. The little creek was joined by another runoff stream and the trail took to the high side on the south slope of the steeper hills. Tall, slender fir stood close to one another, each with humbled branches that took the line of a woman's long skirt and draped to the ground, brushing the needle-covered floor with their thin branches. The trail wove in and out of the trees, offering short glimpses of the valley bottom and timber-covered slopes. The creek knifed its way through the rugged mountains, showing the occasional outcrop that pushed it aside and standing guard at strategic points along the way. One mountainside, with steep, rocky slopes, showed the scars of many avalanches that had cleared the mountain of most of the timber, leaving only bare trails where once stood tall, mature forests.

They rounded another point, another creek joined the first, and the trail pointed the way through thickets of aspen that painted the valley with a ripe green contrast to the black timber of the steep hillside. A little further on and the mountains pushed back, long sloping shoulders with dark green woods of pine and spruce kept the thin fir at bay. The meandering creek, much broader and fuller now and known as the East Fork of the San Juan River, wandered about making its way down the valley floor. Reuben reined up, pointing ahead, "There's some elk. How 'bout some fresh elk liver for supper?"

"Only if you can find a patch of onions to go with it!" declared Elly.

Reuben nodded, grinning, and nudged Blue forward, moving to the side of the valley and hugging the tree line. There was a stretch of trees that sided the river but allowed a grassy meadow about a hundred yards wide and a half-mile long to provide a lazy graze for the herd of elk. As he neared the edge of the trees, Reuben leaned forward, moving side to side to peer through the trees, and turned back to Elly, whispering, "I'm gonna go to ground, hug the trees at the edge of these hills, and try to get a little closer. I'd like to get a young bull, maybe a cow without a calf. You keep the horses quiet."

"Why can't I go get the elk and you keep the horses?" countered Elly, stopping Reuben as he started to step down.

He looked at her with a frown, surprised at her suggestion, then relaxed, smiled, and said, "Why not? You can do it!" and motioned for her to step down and start her stalk. He started to tell her what to do but stopped, knowing she wanted to be trusted and not instructed, so he just accepted the rein of the appy and nodded as he watched her check her Henry and start to the trees. He stepped down, tethered the animals, and let them graze on the fresh spring grasses, and went to the trees to watch his blonde hunter at her stalk.

Elly had a natural ability to move through the woods as quietly as a stalking cougar, carefully picking each step, feeling with her moccasined foot before giving it her weight, and moving without losing sight of her target. She moved at a slow pace but covered the ground quickly as possible and still moved silently. She watched the animals, careful to move only when they were not looking her way, for she knew they could probably smell her or at least something different and would be watching the trees for any predator. The mothers casually stepped between their calves and the trees, cropping the grass, and watching the tree line. There were a few young bulls, none that would be considered a herd bull, and it would be the older cows that led the herd and would be careful to sound any alarm. The cow elk would often make a sharp bark sound to spread the alarm of danger, and Elly wanted to be sure of getting her shot before any alarm would be sounded.

She had traversed about halfway into the length of the meadow, keeping to the trees, and dropped to one knee beside a big ponderosa. She spotted a young bull, spikes in the velvet, and chose him for her target. He was near a big cow with calf, and another yearling bull, but he stood in the clear and she lifted her rifle, using the tree beside her for support. She brought the hammer to full cock, having chambered a round before she left the horses, and lined up the front blade with the *v* sights in the rear. She took a deep breath, let a little out and began to squeeze the trigger. The Henry bucked and spat smoke and lead and the bullet flew true, taking the bull just forward of the upper shoulder, in the neck.

The bull staggered, stumbled to its knees, and dropped his head. The shot had startled the herd and they all moved as if joined at the hip. The alarm bark was sounded and sounded again, and the herd stretched out their long legs and took to the upper edge of the meadow, ducking into the trees around the point of rocks, and disappearing into the deep draw that climbed into the mountains. Elly looked back where the bull had fallen, and he was gone. She looked to the trees and saw the bull stumbling into the woods after the rest of the herd. She shook her head, pursed her lips, and stood, stubbing her foot into the ground in frustration, and started back to the horses.

13 / STORM

Reuben had watched the herd and his woman, always careful to keep her in sight and aware of what was happening. He saw her shot, watched the bull stumble, and the herd stampede into the trees. When the bull came to his feet and staggered after the others, Reuben stepped aboard Blue, snatched up the reins of the appy and the lead of the mule and pushed out of the trees, going for Elly. When she stepped out of the trees, she looked up at her man, her face and neck showing red as she shook her head, "I hit him! I know I did! I saw him go down!" she declared, trotting to Daisy, and slipping her Henry into the scabbard.

She stepped aboard the mare and looked at Reuben as he said, "We'll get him! C'mon!" and nudged Blue toward the mouth of the long draw that pointed to the peak in the northwest. "I don't think he'll go far, he was hit pretty good," he declared. "But I been watchin' those clouds," he turned around in his saddle, pointing to the clouds that were boiling behind the mountain range to the southeast, "and I'm thinkin' last night was just a practice run. I think I heard some thunder comin' from yonder way."

"If that is a storm, we need to get that elk butchered and find some shelter, and I'd like to find somethin' better'n we had last night!" pleaded Elly, scowling at her man.

"You're right about that. This here cut goes clear to the high-up and we can keep a watch for a cave or overhang, somethin' like that." He leaned down for a closer look at the tracks of the scrambling elk, looking for blood sign. He pointed to the tracks, "He's bleedin' good, won't go far." He had no sooner made his declaration, than he looked up the trail and saw the carcass of the elk on the low side of the trail, feet uphill, head in the brush. "There!"

They tethered the animals and started with the elk, splitting the carcass from tail to chin, and laying back the hide as one began the skinning, the other doing the gutting. With the steaming gut pile sliding down the slope below the trail, scavengers were already circling overhead as Bear lay to the side, chewing on a piece of leg bone. They were deboning the meat, piling it on the hide, keeping the choicest cuts and leaving the trimmings and bones for the birds and scavengers. With one big bundle strapped atop the panniers of the mule, two smaller bundles behind the saddles of each horse, the couple swung aboard, accompanied by howling cold winds, to begin their search for shelter.

A quick glance to the sky showed darkening clouds, as thunder rolled over the mountains and the crackle of lightning could be heard. Reuben led the way, pushing up the trail, searching the hillsides and woods for any possible shelter. He looked for overhangs on mountainsides, dark maws that told of a cave, or big downed trees that might have a root ball and thick branches that could be fashioned into shelter. The big horse picked his footing on the narrow trail, following the tracks of the many elk, as Reuben twisted and turned, looking around.

A long flat-topped shadow caught his eye, and he drew to a stop, shaded his eyes, and looked. He pointed to the uphill side of the trail, "I'm gonna check that out. Wait here!" he hollered, making himself heard over the howling wind and distant thunder. He pushed through the trees and saw a long overhang from a steep cliff face, a wide flat bottom, but the overhang was only two to three feet deep and would shelter little. He stepped off Blue, walked into the cliff face and looked around, but as he turned, he caught sight of a dark hole on the opposite hillside. The steep face of the mountain showed what he was certain was a cave. He leaned forward, squinting, and saw what appeared to be a trail that led to the opening, thick brush around the face, but the dark shadow of the cavern showing in the dim light.

He swung back aboard as he shouted to Elly, "There's a cave yonder, looks like a trail, follow me!" and pushed Blue off the trail and into the trees. They crossed the little creek in the bottom, kept his eyes on the rocky abutment that was his landmark, and pointed Blue to the dim game trail. Within moments, they were before the dark maw and Reuben said, "Wait, I'll check it out!" He dropped to the ground to go into the cave entry. He pushed aside the brush, kicking, and clawing to make the entry, then stepped into the black hole. He paused, listening, trying to hear anything from within. He sniffed, searching for the smell of bear or other animal, but there was nothing but the faint odor of charcoal from a long dead fire.

He turned back, fought with the brush, and used his big Bowie knife like a hatchet, and cleared the way to the entry. "It's big enough for us and the horses. Let's get inside!" he declared, grabbing the reins of Blue and starting into the cave. The big roan hesitated, pulled back, but the insistent tug of Reuben won out and they went into the cave. He turned around to see the light at the entry, and called for Elly, "C'mon."

He dropped the reins of the roan, went to help Elly with her horse and the mule and soon all were inside. "I'll get a fire goin', there's some sticks there from some time long past. Once it's goin', I'll go get us some more wood outside and you can help with the horses. We need the wood first 'fore the rain comes," explained Reuben as he stacked the bits and pieces and used a rat's nest for starter. The fire from the lucifer quickly got the flames flaring and with a nod to Elly, Reuben stood and started for the entry.

Reuben dragged a couple snags of dead trees into the cave, went for more and returned with a couple armloads of smaller branches and dropped them in a pile to the side. He looked at the little fire, saw Elly had stripped the gear from the animals and was puttering about to prepare some coffee. He looked about, "I think this is gonna be cozy, don'tchu?"

"Ummhmm," replied Elly, smiling. "But you might get a little more wood, I think it's gonna be cold tonight."

"Alright, alright. You're probably right, and once I get that, I'll need to explore back there a little, make sure there's no bears still hibernatin'!"

"Bears?! You're kidding, right?" she asked, scowling at him.

"Aww, they're probably all out and about anyway, but it won't hurt to check. You can keep watch, so they don't come back. The fire'll probably keep 'em out," he chuckled, grinning at his woman who stood with hands on hips and her head cocked to the side, scowling at him.

With two more trips for wood, the pile had grown and appeared to be sufficient for the night. Reuben stomped his feet, slapped his hands together, and looked to the fire, looking for the coffee pot. Seeing none, he looked to Elly with a questioning look on his face and she giggled and said, "It takes water to make coffee! There's the pot and the waterbag, you might want to get both full 'fore the light fades."

Reuben shook his head, picked up the pot and bag and started for the creek at the bottom of the draw. When he stepped out of the entry, the wind howled and whipped by, cutting his face with the cold and he hunkered his shoulders down, lifted his collar, and started slipping and sliding down the steep slope to get to the water. Once the containers were full, he looked at the clouds, jumped when lightning struck somewhere in the trees near the top of the mountain on the far side, and started clawing his way up the steep slope to get to the cave.

Water crashed down on him as if he had stepped under a waterfall, splattering his face and neck, drenching his heavy wool capote. He staggered into the opening, shaking his head, and removing his hat to shake off the water. He took the pot and bag to the fire, dropped them beside the rocks, and quickly stripped off his capote and wiped off as much water as he could. "Whooeee! That water's comin' down! There's gonna be flash floods all over these mountains! Sure glad we found this cave!" he declared, watching Elly set the coffee pot beside the flickering fire and step back. She had fresh meat simmering over the fire and was busy making biscuits for the Dutch oven.

She looked at Reuben, "You could make a torch with those bigger branches, check out the rest of the cave, make sure there's no varmints back there. I'd hate to get some wild creature hungry smellin' this food and have him come chargin' through here and ruin our supper," she suggested, nodding to the dark interior of the cave.

Reuben chuckled, "Alright, I'll go check to see if there's any boogybears back there!" and went to the woodpile.

The flame sputtered as Reuben lifted the sap-covered pine branch high, letting the circle of light spread before him. The cavern stretched into the darkness as the wind howled and whistled behind him. The torch crackled and spat as the slight breeze of a draft wafted the flame as the air moved along the ceiling of the cavernous passage. The main cavern where the horses and Elly were was about forty feet across with the ceiling as high as twenty plus feet, but the passage narrowed, and walls closed in as the light from the torch illuminated the cavity that was less than half the size of the central space behind him. He paused as the light showed what appeared to be a fork in the passage, with a larger hollow to his right, darkness at the end, and a smaller, about eight feet wide and high, tunnel that branched off on his left. He lifted the torch to peer into the smaller tunnel, saw what he guessed to be a partial cave-in that had water dripping above, leaving the slick accumulation of calcium carbonate that made the formation look like a smooth pile of slick stone. He picked up a rock and threw it past the stalagmite pile into the black hole above. He frowned when he heard the rock strike what sounded like metal.

A cloud of fluttering black wafted from the hole, clicking, clattering, and chirping—the flapping cloud dipped and flew past. Reuben knew he had stirred up a big band of bats as he ducked his head, covering his face and head with his arms. After they passed, he turned to face the larger passage and was jolted to his knees when an explosion of lightning struck somewhere high on the mountain that rumbled and shook the entire cavern. Loose rock tumbled, the torch wavered and Reuben came to his feet, looking around and started back to the main cavern, fearful for Elly and the animals.

The torch sputtered out as he ran the length of the passage, feeling the earthquake rumble as the mountain was struck again. Bits of rock broke from the ceiling and walls, crashing down to worsen the shock of the thunderous strike of lightning. The blast of lightning flashed outside the entrance, illuminating the cavern and Reuben saw the horses and mule jerk back from the shock. Elly stood near the fire and was facing the entry when Reuben called out, "Hit the ground! Cover yourself!" The blast from the lightning echoed into the cavern with a whoosh of air that suffocated the fire, adding darkness upon darkness. Reuben kept moving, flashes of light from outside bolts of lightning briefly illuminated the cavern until he made his way to Elly. He snatched up a blanket and dropped beside her, wrapping them both in the warmth.

"This is gonna get worse 'fore it gets better!" he declared, drawing her close.

She pulled away to look at him, "Oh, you're a big help, and such encouragement. You're supposed to be comforting and protecting. Didn't your mother teach you anything?"

14 / VISITORS

The big Scotsman, Sean McTavish, was the first to roll out after the passing of the windstorm that had played havoc with their sleep. He was hungry and wanted fresh meat, the thought of which drove him to saddle up and go upstream of the smaller fork to hunt for deer or some other tasty wild game. He had gone just over a mile when he spotted movement among the willows and saw one of the big-eared, white-rumped mule deer and he quickly slipped to the ground, dropping to one knee, and using his upraised knee for an elbow rest, he dropped the deer with one shot through the heart. He stood, grinning, and looking around, smug and happy with himself as he walked to the carcass to begin field dressing the animal.

Tall grass reached the bottom of his stirrups as he rode back toward their camp. The morning breeze made the grass wave like the surface of the ocean, reminding him of his homeland by the sea. He smiled at the remembrance, thought of what the other men would think when he rode in with fresh meat, and used his heels to nudge the big horse into a quicker gait. The carcass lay across the rump of the horse, behind the cantle of the saddle, secured with the tie-down straps, but it bounced with the gait of the horse and Sean slowed the animal. He looked toward the camp, frowned, and stood in his stirrups, shading his eyes from the slow rising sun, and shouted, "Indians! Indians!"

He slapped legs to the horse, reached for his Spencer rifle in the scabbard, and leaned low on the neck of the horse, holding his rifle like a pistol. He fired toward the figures in the grass and lay the rifle across the pommel as he charged into the camp. The others were slow in rolling from their blankets, but the shot from the rifle and shout from their friend, brought them to their feet, rubbing their eyes and looking about just as the Indians rose from the grass and started screaming their war cries, launching a barrage of arrows into the camp of the intruders.

The men were quick to bring their rifles to bear and a sudden volley from the rifles of five men, gun smoke boiling along the line, slowed the charge of the Indians. In an instant, the warriors dropped from sight in the tall grass and silence came like a blanket across the lower meadow. Nothing moved, no sound came, no target was seen, and the men searched, exposing themselves as they looked, until an arrow whispered through the tall grass and buried itself in the shoulder of one man that had sought shelter under the wagon. Mickey Lemmon screamed, "I'm hit, I'm hit!"

Patrick Matthews shouted back, "Quiet!" before dropping to his knee behind the wagon then asked, "Where you hit?"

Lemmon was lying on his back, the arrow standing tall with half the shaft showing as the fletching fluttered with his movement. "In the shoulder," he winced, struggling for breath. "What're we gonna do?" he pleaded, trying to look toward the meadow.

"Fight back, what'd you expect? We're fightin' to survive!" answered Matthews, standing to look over the wagon into the meadow.

"I din' expect no Injun war!" groaned Lemmon.

"I think I got one," said Aiden McIntyre, looking at his cousin, Sean.

"I didn't see any of 'em fall, but I was kinda busy," answered Sean.

"There's movement, they're gonna charge again!" squealed Smitty, lifting his rifle. He held a Sharps rifle and a Dragoon pistol lay on the seat of the wagon beside him. "Get ready!" he warned. His words had yet to fall from the air before him when the grassy meadow sprouted feathered and painted warriors that screamed and charged, firing arrows and at least two firing rifles. The men at the wagon answered with another volley that slowed the charge again, but several were still coming as the men fired spasmodically. Some with pistols, others with another round from their rifles, some with Spencers and one with a Henry, but the lead barrage stopped the charge as the warriors went to ground again, now less than thirty yards away.

The firing paused, the men looking and watching for any movement, but the grass waved back revealing nothing. As the men began to breathe a little easier, George Leck suggested, "Maybe they've gone."

"You wanna walk out there an' check?" asked Smitty, chuckling as he spoke.

"You can, I ain't!" answered Leck.

A few moments later Sean said, "Look there, on that slope to the right. Ain't that them? Looks like it to me!"

Patrick Matthews shaded his eyes to look across the

meadow to the shoulder of the foothills. Several riders came from the grassy meadow and started up the slope, none looking back. "I think that's them, but we need to be sure. Sean, how 'bout you and Aiden work your way through the grass and make sure. See if there's any wounded or dead out there."

Sean shook his head as he looked at his cousin, a look that exchanged their similar thoughts about their would-be leader, Matthews, until Sean whispered, "Might as well, ain't nobody else gonna do it. Let's stay close and take it easy." They rose from their cover, pushed their way through the bushes beside the wagon and started into the tall grass. The grass was waist high on the men and they moved at a steady pace, rifles held before them, watchful for any movement. The bodies of two warriors, both on the young side, lay in the grass, blood covering their chests and necks told of similar wounds, but neither stirred and both stared through sightless eyes at the thin clouds above. A quick check of the rest of the meadow within about a hundred yards of their camp showed nothing else alarming, and the cousins turned back to the wagon.

As they walked into camp, Smitty said, "If it hadn't been for Sean givin' the warnin', we'd all be dead men. I think we need to keep a watch from now on, don'tcha reckon?" asking no one in particular but receiving several mumbled responses of agreement.

"I'm all for sinkin' muh teeth into some o' that fresh meat Sean brought in," said Patrick, "And after that, I think we need to get away from here as soon as we can. They might get their friends and come back!"

"How's about somebody helpin' me with this arrow," whined Lemmon. He had crawled from under the wagon and now stood beside the big wheel, his hand on his bloodied chest, holding the arrow still as he looked at the others.

"I'll give ya a hand with that," replied Smitty, slipping his skinning knife from the sheath at his hip and moving closer to the wounded man.

Lemmon's eyes flared wide as he looked at Smitty's knife and expression. As Smitty worked on Mickey, the others set to on the deer, except for Patrick who readied the cookfire and started some coffee. Patrick stepped up on the wagon, stood on the seat and scanned the valley up the south fork of the Rio Grande, looking for any sign of the Indians' return. Seeing none, he returned to the fire and tended the coffee and began whipping up some cornmeal and makings for corn dodgers to fry in the skillet to go with the venison steaks.

The men made short work of their breakfast with the talk turning to both the Indians and the weather. Patrick said, "If we make good time today, we can be well away from the Indians, and I don't think we'll be bothered again. There were about a dozen of 'em this mornin' and we kilt two, wounded others, and I think that'll teach 'em not to mess with us!"

"Unless'n they go to their village and bring back twice as many!" grumbled Smitty, continuing to chew while he talked.

"I'm a mite concerned 'bout them clouds yonder. They're lookin' plumb mean! If'n we was back in Indiana, I'd say that was shapin' up to a tornado, but I don't think these mountains have whirlwinds like that," observed George Leck, nodding to the dark boiling clouds in the south.

"No, but from what I hear, the thunderstorms ain't nuthin' to sit thru in the mountains," added Smitty.

"Well, whether it's Injuns or thunderstorms, either

way, we need to get a move on and hightail it outta here. Maybe we can find better shelter further upstream. At least that way we'll be gettin' closer to our goal on the map!" announced Patrick, rising, and walking to the water's edge to clean his plate and cup with the sand and water.

It was another stop-and-go day with the men changing off as to who would try the panning in each of the creeks and who would do the scouting. They agreed that at least two men should stay with the wagon and two should scout, leaving two with the pans for each of the creeks, but the six men rotated at their tasks, each one eager to be the first to pan color.

The first creek was not much more than a trickle that came from a long draw west of the river and Smitty was the first to try his hand, unsuccessfully. It was another two to three miles before another runoff stream came from the east side of the long valley and it was Patrick Matthews that got his feet wet with the gold pan, but after several attempts and fingering the mud in the pan, washing it around several times, the only glitter he got was some fine bits of mica. But that was the first creek from the east and the second clue on the map of LeBlanc and with that showing progress, Patrick gave up the pan for the reins of the mules as he mounted the wagon. Sean and Aiden, the Scottish cousins, relieved Matthews and Smitty of the panning duties, and Smitty climbed aboard the wagon with Matthews and started south while Sean and Aiden rode the east bank of the river, anxious for a try at the panning.

The river took a tight bend around a tall rocky bluff forcing the panners to the west bank, but it also exposed another small creek that came from high up on the western mountains. The men slipped to the ground, pans in hand and waded into the narrow creek. It was a long cascade that came from high up and dropped with a series of waterfalls before slowing and merging with the South Fork. Sean was on one side, Aiden on the other, as they climbed up the steep hillside, stopping to pan at each little pool that settled below the cascades. A sudden shout from Aiden stopped Sean, making him look back at his cousin who was waving, shouting, and pointing to the pan. Sean splashed across the creek and came beside his cousin, "Look! Look! There's gold!" pointing excitedly at the pan.

Sean took the pan from his cousin, lifted it close to his face, and fingered the silt in the bottom, water sloshing as he moved, and three tiny flakes of gold sparkled in the light. Sean lifted his grinning face to his cousin, "It's gold!" he shouted, just as the first raindrops struck his face and turned his attention to the black clouds boiling overhead.

15 / DISCOVERY

"I'll get the fire goin' again, maybe I'll try to cover the entry to keep out the wind," began Reuben as he rose to his feet and spread the blanket over Elly's still form. She pulled the blanket tight around her and nodded, watching Reuben gather some of the firewood from the pile and lay it near the fire ring. The coals glowed and glimmered in the breeze, dusty ashes flittering about, as he lay more wood on the coals in a crisscross fashion, then on hands and knees, he carefully blew on the embers to bring the fire to life. Hungry flames licked at the wood, filling the cavern with flickering light and dancing shadows. Reuben sat back, glanced to Elly who was up on her elbows and looking at the fire and smiled at her man.

He went to the stack of gear, rummaged through the pile until he found the extra oilcloth ground cover. With a handful of sticks, he went to the opening of the cave to drape the cover over the entry. It was a bit of a fight with the wind and the almost horizontal rain, but by positioning the oilcloth with wedges of wood and forcing it into cracks and crevices and pushing the sticks into the cracks to hold it tight, he finally had it secure. He stood back, satisfied with his work, and returned to the blazing fire. Elly had come from her blankets and nudged the coffeepot closer to the flames and smiled up at her man, "It's gonna get downright cozy in here!"

"We might be here a while. That storm doesn't seem to be letting up any, and even if it does, the runoff water's gonna fill the draws and canyons to an impassable depth." He squatted on his heels, looking at Elly, and added, "When I was back there," nodding to the back of the cavern and the tunnel, "I threw a rock into one branch of the tunnel and I'm pretty sure it hit metal."

"Metal? What would be back in a hole like this that is metal?" asked Elly, frowning.

"Dunno, but I think we should go take a look and find out. Maybe it's just a shovel or something left from a prospector or..." he shrugged, grinning and giving an inviting look of curiosity and mystery.

"Well, you're not leaving me behind, that's for sure!" she answered, glancing at the horses and mule, and down at the sleeping dog. "They're fine and not goin' anywhere, so, let's go!" She stood and extended her hand to help him to his feet.

He grabbed a couple of sappy piñon branches and handed her one, poking his into the fire to get it flaming. Once it flared up, he stepped back and said, "We'll save yours for later," and started into the tunnel. When they approached the fork in the tunnels, Reuben nodded to the right branch and led the way into the dark maw, holding his torch high and feeling Elly's grip on his shirttail. The light bounced off the trickle of water that carved its way down the tunnel toward the big cavern and the opening. They paused, looking, and listening, and the light caught figures carved on the wall, ancient petroglyphs not unlike others they had found in the mountains. They stopped, looked closely at the figures that told of an ancient buffalo hunt, driving the woolly beasts over a cliff and harvesting the carcasses below. Dome huts marked a village and stick figures told of families. The only weapons shown were bows and arrows, and lances.

They continued deeper into the tunnel that soon opened into a cavern, smaller than the one at the entry, but still spacious. Reuben stopped, slowly lifting the torch high, the only sound being the crack and snap of the flame, as they looked at three prone figures on the floor of the cavern. Elly slowly stepped to the side of Reuben as they looked upon the blanket-wrapped forms. Beside the bodies lay bows, quivers of arrows, clay jars, a buffalo robe, a ceremonial headdress, and other personal items, all covered by a thick layer of dust. "They must have been important; you can tell that was quite the headdress," remarked Elly, pointing to the remains of the heavily feathered ceremonial adornment. It was evident that rodents had done their work on the items and blankets and left their tracks and more all over the dusty forms.

The nearest form suddenly moved and both Reuben and Elly jumped back, almost dropping the torch. Reuben held his arm before Elly, she grabbed it tight, as they stood staring and breathless, watching a big rat scurry from under the blanket and disappear into the dark recesses of the cavern. Both exhaled and chuckled as they relaxed, looking at one another, until Reuben said, "How 'bout we check out the other tunnel?"

"I'm all for that!" answered Elly, still giggling at their shock.

They soon returned to the fork of the tunnels and

turned into the smaller of the two, but Reuben's torch fluttered, and he said, "We better light the other one." He reached for the sappy stick carried by Elly. The new torch sputtered and cracked as the flame flared and Reuben lifted it high, dropping the remains of the first to the ground and snuffing it out. "I heard rocks falling when the lightning struck earlier, so it might be collapsed."

He was surprised to see the cave-in had shattered the many stalagmites and stalactites, leaving a jumbled pile of smooth-surfaced remnants mixed with chunks of rock from the roof of the tunnel. Almost all the debris and damage was to the left edge of the passage, leaving a gaping opening to the right with the dark cavernous tunnel beyond. Reuben held his torch closer, jumped back when a large rat scampered over the pile, and chuckled to himself.

Elly giggled, "You jumped like that was a grizzly bear! I thought you were gonna trample me!" poking him in his back to urge him on.

"Well, I didn't expect to see no rat! I hate rats! Almost as much as I hate snakes! Especially when they're as big as a rabbit!" He continued to growl and mumble as he started over the edge of the debris pile, careful to keep the torch before him. He clambered over the rocks, stood on the far side, and held the torch for Elly to see and join him. Once together, they started off again and had gone just a few feet when he stopped, looking into the poorly lit tunnel and saw a glimmer of light that he thought was a reflection. He leaned forward, extending the torch, and walked slowly on, careful to watch each step and any other possible dangers.

The floor of the tunnel appeared to rise, the ground covered with a thick layer of dust and loose dirt. To the side, something seemed to shine and Reuben bent to one knee, holding the torch forward and close to the smooth surface. He reached out and wiped some of the dirt and dust free, surprised to see smooth, shiny metal. He wiped more off, feeling the slight contour of the metal, and pulled at it, freeing it from the dirt, and fell back with the exertion, dropping the torch. Elly quickly grabbed the torch off the ground, holding it high to let it flare and light the cavern. Reuben held an ancient breastplate, dulled and dirty with accumulated grime and more, but it was easy to see what had been shining and sounding like metal.

Reuben frowned as he looked at it, turning it over and moving it around to see all sides and angles. He fingered the strapping that crossed over the shoulders and came together at the lower chest. He held it before him and said, "Whoever he was, he wasn't very big!" He pointed to the lower edge, "This barely covers my chest, and exposes my belly. But if the wearer was shorter, smaller maybe, it would cover him to his waist, maybe more." He held it out before him, glanced at Elly and said, "This is French. They were called Cuirassiers, cavalry men. But it was late 1700s when the French came through here!" He shook his head and began looking around for other items, thinking there might be more pieces of the armor. Just past where the breastplate had lain, he saw what he thought was a stack of rock and nudged one with his foot. He frowned and said to Elly, "Hold that torch closer here," pointing to the pile. He grabbed one of the rocks, lifted it and said, "That's heavy," and examining it, added, "and this ain't no rock!" He slipped his Bowie from the sheath at his back and using the tip of the blade, began scratching at the surface of the stone. He looked at Elly, "Bring the torch closer."

She stepped closer, lowered the torch near his hands with the rock. Neither moved nor even breathed for a moment until Reuben whispered, "That's gold!" He hefted the rock, noticed it was flat on one side, rounded on the other, and said, "That's the shape of a lead pot, you know, like we use for melting lead for balls for the pistols. It's bigger than what we use, but that's what it was! They melted down gold, did their own refining, made these balls or whatever you call them." He hefted it again, dug a little deeper with his knife and smiled, "But why didn't they take it with them?"

He walked to the pile, noted it was more than knee-high and at least ten feet long as they were stacked against the wall of the tunnel. "That's why, there's so many it'd take a couple wagons or several pack animals." Reuben shook his head at the realization of the amount of gold that lay before him. "And each one of these is about five or six pounds! That makes each one of these worth about $1,500!"

"So? We don't need it, we've got money sittin' in the bank that we haven't touched and don't need, so what would we do with that much money?" asked Elly, showing her frustration and concern.

"You're right, we don't need it, but..."

"But what?" she asked, frowning.

Reuben looked at the ingot in his hand, looked at the long pile, and back to Elly. "We don't need it, and it should stay here, but I say we take two, one in your packs, one in mine. Stash 'em in the bottom and forget about 'em but know they're always there if we need it."

"One each!" she agreed, holding up one finger and cocking her head to the side, showing a slight squint to her eyes as she glared at Reuben.

He chuckled, picked up another ingot, tucked the

armor under his arm and turned back to return to the main cavern. Elly followed close behind, holding the torch high to light the way over Reuben's shoulder, and mumbled as she walked.

"What're you sayin'?" he asked, turning to face her.

"Just wonderin' what you're gonna do with that armor," she answered, watching him climb over the rock pile. He stood on the far side, reached across to accept the torch from Elly and answered, "Dunno. Might trade it to the Mouache, they always like to have things like this, or, might keep it! Wear it to church so the preacher's sermon won't get me!"

Elly picked up a small rock and chucked it at Reuben's back, hitting him square between the shoulders. "Ouch! What'd you do that for?"

"Tryin' to knock some o' that meanness out and some good sense in!" mumbled Elly.

Wind whipped at the mouth of the cave, snapping the oilcloth as it clung to the rocks. Lightning flashed and scratched at the storm-darkened sky, splitting the blackness with spiderwebs of fire as the thunder crashed, echoing across the canyons, bouncing over the peaks. Rain fell in torrents, runoff already cascading down every draw and ravine. Floodwaters roared from the canyon floor, crashing and smashing against cliff walls, carrying uprooted trees, carcasses of animals, and pushing walls of mud and silt like a crawling ogre that consumed everything in its path. Massive boulders, loosened by the incessant and unceasing downpour, rumbled from high mountains, smashed through ancient growths of pine and aspen, leaving in its wake a slow growing mudslide that would carry any survivors to an early grave.

Reuben built up the fire, dared to push aside the

entry covering and was blasted with the torrential forces of the mountain downpour. He fought against the gale to secure the oilcloth and turned back to the fire with water dripping from his clothes. He stood, hands outstretched to the flames and warmth, shaking his head, "Everything about these mountains is going to be different come daylight, if it comes! I've never seen a storm like this, ever!"

Elly stood and came to the side of her man, wrapping her arms around his waist and laying her head against his chest. She turned her face up to his and said, "Whatever comes, I'm glad we're together!"

Reuben smiled, drew her close and bent to kiss her. As they embraced, the horses stamped their feet, snorted, and sidestepped, nervous because of the storm. Both Elly and Reuben went to their horses, stroked their necks and heads, talking softly, to comfort them and assure them of their presence. The animals settled down and Reuben returned to the fire, reached for the coffee pot and cups, poured them some coffee, and said, "Well, we've got food, coffee, and warmth. What more can we ask for?"

"How 'bout some quiet so we can get some sleep?" answered Elly, accepting the offered coffee, and smiling at her man. "It's going to be a long night and I'm not sure we'll even see daylight, come morning, but I'm all for getting some rest," she suggested, reaching down to stroke the thick fur of Bear who lay at her feet.

16 / CANYON

The raindrops felt like ice. Patrick Matthews hunkered down into his mackinaw and pulled the hat down in an effort to keep the cold water from reaching his neck. Slapping reins to the mules he searched for any place for shelter. With a glance to the dark clouds that seemed to be chasing him up the canyon, he turned slightly to face Smitty, "Look for some cover, trees, rocks, anything! I think this storm's gonna get bad in a hurry!"

The mules leaned into the traces, digging deep with their hooves, as Patrick slapped reins to their rumps and shouted his commands. Smitty put a hand to his hat, fearful of losing his head covering, and struggled to see as the rain grew heavy. He leaned to the side, looking to the right where the steep shoulder of the mountain pushed toward the river, leaving an alluvial sweep that had grown tall with big spruce and cottonwoods near the water. He pointed to the tall trees, shouted, "There!"

Patrick looked, squinting through the rain and wind, nodded, and pulled hard on his left hand full of wet reins. The mules ducked their heads, leaned to the left and crashed through the brush, aiming for the shelter of the big trees. He leaned back, pulling taut the reins, and bringing the mules to a stop beside a big rough-barked cottonwood. He looked about, turned to Smitty, who was hunkered into his coat, and pointed to the thicket of trees, "You get some firewood, we're gonna need plenty! Stack it under the wagon! I'll tend to the mules and get a shelter started." He tied off the reins and climbed down from the wagon and began unhooking the mules.

The wind was picking up and whistling through the pines, cottonwoods rattled their leaves and the trees bent to the will of the storm. Boiling clouds turned dark, churning, and stirring, loosing their baggage of water and the strength of the storm increased, but still it was tolerable, as the men worked to prepare their camp. Patrick dragged the biggest tarp from the stack of gear and supplies in the wagon. He tested the tie-downs on the oilcloth that covered their supplies and tossed the big tarp to the ground. Dropping down beside it, he began tethering the tarp to the top boards of the wagon, stretching out the big covering and letting it lie as he went in search of saplings sufficient to use as tent poles to keep the peak of the tarp high to shed water.

As Smitty dropped an armload of wood under the wagon, the two Scotsmen rode into the camp and slipped to the ground beside their mounts. Their coats wet, hats drooping, the grins of the men went unnoticed by the other two men as Patrick glanced up and hollered, "We need tent poles, quick! Gotta get a shelter up 'fore the worst o' that storm hits!" The wind competed with his words as it began to howl and scream through the trees, but the cousins heard and began stripping their horses of the gear. Saddles and more would be stashed under the wagon and the men dropped their gear just under the wagon box.

With the help of the Scots, the canopied tarp was up and tightly secured with the wagon and ground ties, allowing just enough room for the six men to roll out their blankets and have a secure shelter from the storm. Patrick stood to the side, sheltered under the tall spruce and looked at their makeshift cover. “Looks like it’ll do!” he declared, looking to the cousins.

Sean said, “Dunno, that wind is already poppin’ and snappin’ that tarp. If it gets worse, it might just take flight and blow away.”

“Nah, I think these trees will be ‘nuff of a break to protect the camp,” added Smitty, looking around, “But I wanna know where we’re gonna have a fire for some coffee! I can handle just ‘bout anythin’ longs I got some java!”

“There’s another tarp, smaller’n that ‘un, in the wagon. Maybe we can make a lean-to or somethin’ here ‘mong the trees so we can have a fire,” suggested Patrick.

“Then let’s get to it!” declared Smitty, starting for the wagon and the tarp and firewood.

A short while later, George Leck and Mickey Lemmon rode into camp, drenched and fussing. The two men had been on scouting duty and had been further upstream on the south fork of the big river, deeper into the canyon, and had experienced the howling winds and downpour of the storm in the close confines between cliff faces. They dropped to the ground and began stripping the gear from the horses, Mickey taking the leads of both and going to the trees where the other animals were tethered. When the men saw the fire under the lean-to, they quickly joined the others and poured themselves some coffee. After the first draught, Mickey looked around at the camp, “Good thing you made camp here, it’s a narrow canyon further up the river and there’s no place like this for a camp. The trail sides the river and often dips into the shallows. We went as far as we could before the rain got heavy, so we turned back. We’ll have to wait for this to let up ‘fore we go any further.” He shook his head, took another sip, lifted his eyes to the sky that showed between the trees and saw nothing but black-bellied clouds. “I’m not likin’ the look o’ them clouds!” he declared, looking to the others.

“Well at least in these mountains there ain’t gonna be no twisters!” offered Smitty, sitting on his haunches, savoring the steaming brew in his cup.

“How you know that?” asked George Leck. He was from the flatlands of Indiana and had weathered many a tornado or its like and had no knowledge of the mountain weather.

“Ain’t no twister can form in these mountains. Them hills keep ‘em at bay,” explained Smitty. “But what’chu gotta watch out fer is them thunderbolts, they’ll fry ya in a heartbeat!” he added, nodding to the black clouds. As he nodded, a bolt of lightning struck somewhere beyond the nearest hills, but the flare of light, the upper end of the bolt, and the blast of the strike made everyone jump and a couple spill their coffee. Smitty counted after the lightning, listening for the thunder, made it to fifteen and looked around at the men, “The worst is yet to come, but it’s only three miles away, just beyond them hills yonder.” The rolling thunder seemed to shake the leaves on the cottonwoods and each man was certain he felt the lightning shake the very earth they stood upon.

None of the men had been in a thunderstorm in the mountains. Although Smitty had been around longer, he had never experienced the wrath of nature in the high country. He had heard of such things as flash floods, but until a man has experienced the phenomenon, it is difficult to imagine. The mountains that stood so tall and appeared as the flexed muscles of all of nature, appeared invincible, but the force of nature as designed by the Creator, is beyond the ability of man's mind to conceive.

As they stood together under the big spruce, the lean-to popping in the wind behind them, the men grew silent, their mindless mutterings silenced by the growl of the coming storm. The wide branches of the big spruce dipped in the wind, shaking the water from its needles and showered the men, causing each one to jump back, holding their cups that had caught half their fill with rainwater. The excess drowned the fire, and the parade of wet prospectors quickly dove into the cover of the wagon side shelter.

As Smitty crawled toward his blankets, he mumbled, "Might as well try to sleep, shore cain't do much else!"

As Sean and Aiden crawled into their blankets, Sean looked at Aiden with a questioning look and chuckled, encouraging Aiden to share his news. The men sat on their blankets, hunkered over because of the low ceiling of the cover, and Aiden began, "So, 'fore the storm came, me'n Sean here were doin' some pannin' on that creek that came from the west down that steep slope. You remember seein' the one with all them little waterfalls like?"

Patrick said, "I remember that one, it was right after we gave you two the pans."

"Ummhmm. Well, we started pannin' and climbin' and about a hunert feet up the hill I panned a little pool at the bottom o' one o' them little falls, and..." he chuckled, looking around at the others, "I found color!" He smiled as the others grew excited and began peppering him with questions, "Tweren't much, just three or four flakes, but it *was* color! Sean looked at it and he agreed. So at least we found some gold, maybe there's more!"

The men began jabbering among themselves, talking of gold and riches but remembering the work it took to extract enough gold to make it worthwhile. Sean voiced their concerns when he said, "We gotta remember, it could be just a small pocket and prove to be nothin'. But what we came on this expedition for was not a little pocket of gold in a stream but a fortune in gold stashed away somewhere in these mountains!"

The mutterings of agreement stifled any real discussion as the men remembered the purpose of their journey. Mickey turned to Patrick and asked, "Say, can we have another look at that map, since we're confined to quarters, prisoners of this storm? Maybe we can get a better idea how close we are to the spot!"

Patrick glanced around at the others, turned to dig the map from his saddlebags that lay beneath the saddle he used for a pillow, and brought it forth, unrolling the parchment under the light of the lone lantern. He began explaining the markings, "See, this is the fork in the river where we camped last night and met up with the Indians this morning. And this," pointing at a squiggly line that came from the left edge of the map, "is the first of the three creeks that come from the east. We passed one this mornin' and I think the second one is just across the river, here." He pointed to the map then pointed to the direction of the wagon and the river beyond.

Sean saw an emblem on the map, frowned, and asked, "What's that, that red flower lookin' thing," pointing to the line showing the south fork of the river, past the last creek and nearer the mark of the treasure.

"That's a *fleur-de-lis* or flower of the lily. That's sometimes used by the French to denote royalty or the property of royalty, but sometimes it just means a lily. On the map, it might be a sign or carving left by the French expedition to mark the place of the gold or…" he shrugged.

"I ain't never seen no red lily!" declared Smitty. "White ones, but not red'uns."

"So, it could be a carving on a tree or a mark on a rock or something like that? Something to show where to go, maybe?" asked Aiden.

Patrick nodded, "Perhaps, we'll just have to wait till we get there."

"What's that other thing, up from the lily?" asked Sean, pointing to the map.

Patrick looked at the emblem above the *fleur-de-lis* and pointed at the marking, "This?"

"Yeah, that," answered Sean, nodding his head.

"Since that's on the line of a stream," he ran his fingers along a thin meandering line, "I believe that to be a waterfall. By the looks of the emblem, it would be a big one."

"Now that should be easy to find, even though we've seen a few already."

"Yeah, but wait till you get in that canyon, there's quite a few more in there," explained Mickey Lemmon, glancing to George Leck who had scouted with him and saw the other waterfalls. Both men looked back to Patrick who shrugged and looked back to the map.

17 / DELUGE

The storm came with a fury. Everything leading up to this point was nothing compared to the onslaught of nature's wrath. Wind howled and screamed with the wail of a banshee, trees bent to the will of the wind, some snapped off while others were uprooted and lay wounded among the stronger like casualties on a battlefield. A big cottonwood groaned and creaked, breaking with a splintering crack that made the veterans of the war jump in fear as the big tree slowly split in the middle, the bigger part of the trunk tumbling down to crash on the wagon, splintering the sideboards, smashing the seat and breaking the tailgate as it shattered the boxes of supplies and tools. The front axle splintered, both wheels tipped inward against the box and groaned as the wagon sagged, dropping the oilcloth covering onto the huddled figures underneath.

Lemmon jumped, shouted, "What's happening?"

"A tree fell!" answered Smitty, motioning the man to come to the high side of the shelter. "What if another one falls?" pleaded the man as he tried to crawl to the other side, searching the dark interior with frightened eyes.

"Crawl under the wagon if'n ya want, it might protect ya!" answered Smitty, shouting to be heard above the storm. He motioned to the wagon just as lightning crashed somewhere close above them on the mountain-side and thunder blasted, rolling down into the deeper canyon and echoing back as it penetrated the depths of darkness. Above them, another thunder, lesser than the first, started and slowly gained, adding the roar of cascading water and rolling stones crashing into the woods, breaking, and ripping trees from the ground, pushing a wall of mud and stone that roared and rumbled with a life of its own, competing with the cacophony of the thunderbolts and wailing winds. The massive rockslide tore away at everything in its path, taking boulders, escarpments, slide-rock, and rumbling stone and mud toward the valley bottom. As it crossed the trail and smashed into the timber on the shoulder, it slowly came to a stop, but the rumble of the destruction bounced across the valley as if shouting its triumph over nature itself.

The men had frozen in place, eyes wide and fear painting itself on their alarmed faces—fright filling their innards, confusion muddling their minds. When the roar subsided, they moved, Sean McTavish crawling under the broken wagon, looking about in the downpour, seeing trees that had stood tall and unmoving when they made camp and were seeking shelter under the giants of the wood, were now lying flat, mortally wounded, and unmoving even in the unrelenting storm. He shook his head, grabbed at the sideboards to pull himself up, and looked about, stunned at the destruction and the continuing onslaught of the storm. His cousin stood beside him, and Sean pointed to the trees, a massive spruce that stood, arms outstretched as if taunting the force of nature, and hollered to his cousin, "Let's go there!" and started to the trees.

They looked around, trying to see across the river and the hillside beyond but it was masked by the downpour that was almost horizontal with the ground. The massive pile of trees, rocks, mud, and more from the landslide blocked the view of the canyon, but the crashing of the water in the river was continuous but changing. Sean frowned, looked at Aiden, and said, "Is the river still moving or did that dam it up?"

Aiden frowned as he leaned toward the river, "No, it's runnin', but I think it's gettin' louder!" Both men were yelling to be heard as Aiden followed Sean into the thicker trees. They dropped into a crouch and ducked under the low-hanging limbs of the biggest spruce, went to the trunk and sat with their backs to the big tree. It would not keep them dry, but it was as much protection as the flapping and snapping oilcloth and the wagon.

They sat silent, listening, watching, and feeling the ground tremble beneath them, fearful of what was yet to come. Sean frowned, looking about, stood, and looked up the hill behind the camp and beyond the trail. The crack of a thunderbolt roared and rumbled through the valley, the light showing the beginning of a cascade of water coming down the path of the landslide. White water crashed and splashed, the roar of the water bouncing across the hillsides, and Sean shouted, "Flood! Flood!" pointing up the hill.

Aiden jumped to his feet, came from under the big branches and looked up the hill where Sean pointed. He twisted around, looking at the shelter and shouted to the men, "Get out! Flood coming!" and saw the movement under the shelter. As they looked back up the hill, a bigger roar rumbled from the canyon mouth and Sean instantly knew there was a greater threat coming from the river. He slapped his cousin on the shoulder, pointed to the uphill side of the sloping plain, and they started running through the trees, moving up the slight hill and away from the path of the flashflood.

The surging water of the swollen river was already lapping at the wheels of the wagon as the men crawled from under the tarp. Smitty looked at the water, started for the tethered horses and mules, "C'mon! The horses!" he shouted. Patrick Matthews ducked his head to the deluge and followed after the running Smitty. They ripped the tethers from the trees, slapped the animals on the rear to chase them to the trees and into the wider part of the valley, hoping they could find high ground and some cover.

Smitty and Patrick turned to look at the wagon and the two men fighting their way free of the tarp. Water surged around the wheels, already at the hub and the wagon rocked with the force of the floodwaters. Smitty pulled on Patrick's arm, "Let's get to high ground!" pointing to the trees and the backs of the Scotsmen disappearing into the pines. Patrick followed but as they approached the big timber, he turned and saw the wagon tip over, burying the tarp and bedrolls under the churning water and boiling foam. He looked quickly for the two men and saw nothing. He turned and hollered to Smitty, "They're gone—under water!" pointing back to the camp and the rolling water with debris, mud, and more tumbling with the roiling muddy mass.

The roar of the waters, the repeated thunderbolts, and the howling of the wind was incessant and unrelenting. The men crashed through the brush, fleeing the rising waters, darkness retreating only when the lightning lanced through the darkness with bolts of white fire that fractured the black wall of torrential downpour. They staggered from tree to tree, always looking over their shoulder as the goblins of fear and death chased after them, screaming their taunts and crying their torments accompanied by the whistling and wailing of the imagined hobgoblins that flew among the thickets.

Lightning struck the tallest tree on the alluvial shoulder, splitting it to its roots, sending flaming shards and flying pieces in every direction. The split spruce birthed a flame that licked at the downpour, sputtering and spitting back with every drop, but the storm soon claimed its own and snuffed the flames, leaving the stench of brimstone in the wet air that wailed through the valley.

Once clear of the trees and on higher ground, Sean and Aiden dropped to their bellies in the wet grass that lay prone and humbled from the force of the deluge. They rolled to their backs, covered their eyes as they looked to the boiling bellies of black clouds that continually belched bolts of fire and rolled with thunder making the men feel as if they were being run down by the chariots of the gods. Patrick and Smitty soon dropped down beside them, sitting on the wet ground, and looking back where their camp had been.

A wall of water had rumbled down the canyon, taking everything in its path and continued to surge and roll as more and more water cascaded down the mountains. Every draw, every ravine, every arroyo carried its share and more of the torrent, each one building and growing as it came down the mountains to join the big river that was earning its name as the Rio Bravo del Norte, the grand river of the north. The men were breathing heavy, Patrick stood, shading his face as he tried to look into the still standing trees, the tops of which were all that could be seen, looking for any sign of the two men left behind, but nothing showed. He looked downstream and knew it was hopeless to find anything in that raging inland sea that marched to the north and east. He thought of the main branch of the river, knowing it was more than twice the size of the south fork, and shook his head at the thought of how much water was roaring into the flatlands beyond.

He dropped back to sit down with the other men, head drooping as he said to the others, "I think George and Mickey didn't make it."

The others looked at one another, down to the river and back, and sat silent, knowing it could have been one or more if not all of them. They had made camp too near the river and at the base of a steep mountain with a runoff-carrying draw. They would know better next time, if there would be a next time.

18 / AFTERMATH

Elly awoke to the crackling of the fire, embers rising to dance along the roof of the cavern and drop into the darkness. She rolled to the side to look at Reuben and frowned. "What're you doing?" She rose to one elbow and flipped the covers back as she looked at the fire. "I can tell that's not breakfast," she added, waiting for his explanation.

"I'm melting the gold. Gonna pour it into the bullet molds. I remembered we was still carryin' both the .36 caliber ball mold for your Colt and the .44 caliber ball mold for my Remington. So, what I'm gonna do is mold the gold into the .36 caliber, then drop them into the lead for the .44. That way, we'll be carrying what looks like lead balls, but they'll be solid gold on the inside!" explained Reuben, watching the molten gold in the crucible.

She rose from her blankets and went to his side by the fire, watching him pour some of the molten gold into the mold for the .36 caliber ball. He set the crucible aside, propping it carefully to keep from spilling, lifted the mold, examined the sprue, and opened the mold to drop the balls on the flat rock he had pulled close. He repeated the action until all the gold had been molded, then started on trimming the sprue from the balls. Elly watched, fascinated, as Reuben repeated the action with the second half-round of gold, melting it and molding it. Once he had trimmed all the sprue and made certain of each ball's trim and smoothness, he melted some galena and with the smaller ball in the mold, poured in the lead and shook the mold slightly as he did, letting the molten lead flow beneath the gold ball. When he trimmed the sprue and opened the mold, shiny lead balls fell out and he looked up at Elly, grinning and satisfied.

"Well, as soon as you get done cookin' gold, I'll see if I can get breakfast started. I thought you would at least have the coffee going before you did all that," nodding to the molding gear.

"I was just a little excited about doin' this, so I got started right away. Thankfully, it worked just like I thought so now, instead of a heavy weight in the bottom of the pack, we can have different pouches of balls throughout our gear. And since we use paper cartridges, we won't be gettin' them mixed up."

"I'd hate to think of you having to do that with that entire stack back yonder!" she laughed.

He chuckled at the thought and began gathering up his gear to make way for the meal preparation. He filled the coffee pot from the trickle of water that came from deep within the tunnels, seeing the crystal clear and very cold water as little different from the runoff water that would now be nothing but mud and sludge. He set the pot on the rock next to the flames and sat back, watching Elly prepare some johnnycakes to go with the thin strips of elk meat that hung over the fire, broiling on the sticks.

The storm had let up in the early hours of morning

and was now a steady drizzle, although the sun was trying to make itself known with light making the mountain across the valley appear as a silhouette, framed by the bright haze that danced across the rugged ridge. The roar of runoff was heard as it cascaded down the canyon, carrying storm debris as it crashed through the narrow gorge. The dribble of smaller rivulets that came from the high points of the mountain above them, beat a steady pattern as it fought its way through the trees and buck brush that had covered the mountainside below the bare limestone and granite of the mountain peaks that stood proudly above timberline.

Reuben went to the mouth of the cave, pushed aside the oilcloth, and looked outside. The steady drizzle continued, but was less than the night before, and the wind had abated, making it possible to see through the downpour and know that daylight was coming. Yet he also knew it was not just the storm, but every snowdrift that lay in the shadows, every overhanging cornice of ice and snow at the crest of ridges and every deep drift or glacier in the high country would have been melted under the onslaught of the storm and their water content added to the floodwaters. He turned back to the fire, "I think it'll prob'ly let up later on, maybe by midday. But it'll be a while before we can leave, what with everything so wet, we'd do nothin' but slip and slide, bog down, break a leg, or more. If the sun comes out and warms things up, maybe dries it out a mite, we can prob'ly get out come tomorrow mornin'."

"Tomorrow?"

"Ummhmm, tomorrow. That'll give us time to clean our weapons, check the rest of our gear and make any repairs, maybe catch up on some sleep," he grinned, winking at her with mischief showing in his eyes.

She tore off a piece of the johnnycake and threw it at him, which he caught deftly and took a bite, grinning. She shook her head, giggling at her man and continued with her preparations.

THE FOUR MEN HAD HUDDLED TOGETHER, SITTING BACK-to-back, drawing warmth from one another as the freezing rain continued to fall throughout the night. In a final act of desperation, they climbed together up the tree-covered slope, searching for any break in the storm, anything that would offer some protection, until Smitty called out, "Over here! C'mon, over here!" The three men that had spaced out along the steep slope, turned, and struggled over the slippery rocks, making their way to where Smitty waited. As they neared, he hollered again, "There!" pointing to a rugged escarpment that appeared to be held in place by the exposed roots of a scraggly piñon, wooden tentacles clinging to the jumbled rocks that hung over the trees like the bulbous nose of some prehistoric monster. Under the overhang it was almost dry, the only water that had access was when the wind had whipped the storm about like the prey of a mountain lion trying to break the neck of its quarry.

"And look! There's some dry, well almost dry, wood. Maybe we can get a fire goin'!" declared the whiskery-faced, wiry little man. The men had been careful to keep their rifles and any sidearms with them, even when they crawled from under the oilcloth shelter, and they now stood the rifles against the stone face and helped gather the sticks to start a fire. Within moments, using the well-protected, wrapped in a scrap of oilcloth, lucifers that Smitty always had handy, they soon had a fire going and their spirits lifted. There's something about a warm campfire in the wilderness that offers a camaraderie never found elsewhere. Men become compatriots, even though strangers before, the warmth of a fire that pushes back the darkness and the storms of life, brings a kinship previously unknown.

Smiles began to split faces and plans began to be formed. "First, we'll need to find the horses and mules. I don't think there's any salvaging the wagon, but with the mules, we can still make do, that is if we can find any of the supplies," suggested Patrick.

"Right 'bout now I'd be happy just to find muh bedroll!" offered Smitty as he looked around the circle of men who nodded their agreement.

"How long you think it'll take for the water to go down?" asked Sean, looking from man to man.

"No tellin'. I reckon it depends on when this cussed drizzle lets up, an' then it'll still take a while for all the water to leave the high country," said Smitty, the only one that had been in the mountains before, even though it was only one time. He looked at Patrick, frowned, "Say, what about that there map? Did you think to get it outta the tent?"

Patrick let a slow grin paint his face and he patted his chest. "In here," he answered, motioning to the thick coat and all that was underneath. "I would as soon forget my head as to forget the map, and yes, it's nice and dry," he added.

The others nodded, showing their relief. Sean looked to the sky, saw the colors changing in the east and said, "We might get some sunshine soon. Here's hopin' anyway," nodding to the eastern horizon. From their position high up on the mountainside, they looked northeast down the canyon of the south fork and saw the black of night lifting its curtain to give way to the crowding grey of early morning. Even with the continuing drizzle, the light offered the hope of a new day.

Sean picked up a twig, broke it into four pieces and held them out to the others. "The two shortest go huntin' the horses. The other two will go swimmin' for supplies. If the storm lets up we'll meet down yonder at the tree line, if not, we'll come back up here. The way I see it, we can't spend all day up here with no food and no coffee just waitin' and killin' time. And we can't let them animals get so far away we'll never catch 'em. If the swimmers can't get to anything, then they'll join the others in the horse hunt. Sound 'bout right?" he asked, looking from man to man, seeing each one nod agreement. He held out his hand and offered the sticks, each one pushed up to the same height, about a half-inch above his finger, and let Patrick have the first pick. When all the picks were made, Sean and Aiden had the short ones, and with a nod to the others, started down the hill, shoulders hunkered up to keep the rain out of their collars, and started their search for the animals.

"Do you think we can find anything?" Smitty asked Patrick as they started back to the trees.

"All we can do is try. I think the worst of the flood water might have passed and maybe the wagon's still there. If so, we might get some supplies outta the box," answered Patrick, slipping, and sliding down the rocky and wet slope.

Smitty mumbled some response just as his feet slipped out from under him and he dropped to his rump, holding his rifle high and sliding down the hillside, feet kicking at the rocks and roots, hollering something unintelligible, but prompting Patrick to laugh at his partner until the man came to a stop against a big boulder and struggled to get back to his feet. As Patrick came even with him, he looked at Smitty and said, "You might wanna jump in the water to get rid of about twenty pounds of mud!" chuckling as he nodded to his mud-caked friend.

"Only twenty? More like fifty!" growled the older man, shaking his head and wiping some of the mud off his britches. "This ain't gonna be no fun atall! Not atall!" he grumbled as he followed Patrick to the trees.

19 / ROUNDUP

Floodwaters are the Creator's way of cleaning house. The waters washing down the mountains, taking with them the debris, trash, pine needles, matted leaves, deadwood, and more, usually piling them up at some bend in the river, only to dry out and later be used as firewood for some wilderness wanderer, can easily be seen as the Creator's spring cleaning. When the storm passes and the skies clear, it is a warm, bright, spring sunshine that bathes the land, urging new growth to decorate the world of the wilderness with shades of green. Soon, splashes of color will compete with one another as blossoms stretch to hoard the life-giving sunshine.

As the men walked down the slope of the steep hillside, the rising sun reached forth to turn off the storm's faucet and begin its work of drying out the waterlogged land. As they approached the riverbank, the drizzle lessened to sprinkles and soon the sun peeked through and began to warm the land. Sean and Aiden stopped, lifted their heads to the sky, shaded their eyes and let a smile cross their faces, relieved that the rising sun promised a warmer and dryer day. Sean looked at Aiden, "I'm thinkin' we'll find the animals not too far from the river." He nodded to the riverbank where willows lay flat, mud, silt, and debris intermingled with the thin branches. "Even though it's a mess, just the sound of running water attracts the animals. They'll be lookin' for graze," he motioned to the flats with buffalo grass and greasewood struggling to right themselves, "somethin' tastier than that!"

"Aye, then you stay nigh the water an' I'll walk along the shoulder there," replied Aiden, pointing to the hills on the north side, "and stay high 'nuff to see into the trees and further down the river."

Sean looked to the sky again, "I'm hopin' this is no just a turadh. I'm tired of bein' drookit!" He shook his arms to rid the jacket of some of the water, his actions obvious he had reached the end of his patience with the storm and was anxious for it to be done.

Aiden also looked above and said, "No, to my thinkin' it's not just a break, and I'm tired of bein' wet too. So, let's find the horses and get on with it." He chuckled, realizing the two of them had lapsed into the vernacular of their home country.

"Aye," resolved Sean and looked to the river. As Aiden started to the hillside, Sean stepped to water's edge and looked up and downstream, seeing the evidence of high water and saw the level had already dropped considerably. He looked across the river to see more of the same debris and damage, saw what appeared to be a carcass of some wild animal entangled with the driftwood piled on the high side of a bend in the river and turned his eyes downstream, following the far riverbank to see more of the same. He leaned forward to try to see around the bend on the near side and turned back to follow the river downstream. The grass was wet, the ground boggy, and footing uncertain, making Sean look at the ground before him as much as the brush and foliage along the river.

A break in the trees and shrubs, showed the water still raging past, the roar of the flow bouncing back from the steep cliffs on the far side. He stepped to the opening, made a quick scan of the banks, and started to turn away until something off-color caught his eye. He frowned, looked at the pile of driftwood and debris, and saw what looked like a part of a blanket or piece of clothing. He pushed aside some willows to work his way closer and as he drew near, the object began to take form. A body was entangled in the rubble and as he drew nearer, he saw the familiar pattern of a checkered shirt, torn and ripped, revealing the back of a man. "Mickey," he whispered as he grabbed at the branches of the downed cottonwood. He leaned his rifle against a big boulder on the bank and went to breaking branches and tossing them aside, trying to get to the form of their companion. As he reached for the man's arm to pull his body closer, he felt the resistance of a pullback. "Mickey! Mickey! It's me, Sean!" he hollered to be heard above the roar of the water. He took a tentative step on a grey snag of a log to get closer and reached for the man's belt. He pulled as he said, "Mickey! I'm gonna get you out!" and struggled to pull the man free. Within moments, he dragged the waterlogged form from the driftwood pile and lay him on the wet, grassy bank. He dropped to his knees beside him, gasping for breath from the exertion.

Mickey was struggling to breathe, choking on everything he had swallowed in his fight for life, and Sean rolled him to his side to begin pounding on his back to help him expel the mess. Finally, Mickey breathed deep, coughed, sucked air again, and rolled to his back, exhausted but relieved to see blue sky above him. He turned to look at his rescuer, "Did you see George?" he growled with a raspy voice, frowning.

"No! We were lookin' for horses. We thought you and George were lost in the flood!"

"We were…together…held on…but the water…" he choked, looking at Sean.

"We didn't have any hope for either of you, you're almighty lucky to have washed up here. George is prob'ly halfway to Kansas by now."

Sean stood, helped Mickey to his feet, and with the waterlogged man hanging onto his shoulder, Sean walked from the brush into the open space of the roadway, just as Aiden came riding up, grinning broadly, as he sat on his big bay horse, the leads of others in his hands and the four mules, leads tied to tails, followed after. "Found 'em all! They was standin' hipshot in the bright sunshine, dryin' off and were as happy to see me as I was to find them!" declared Aiden. He spotted Mickey on the far side of Sean and frowned, "Where'd you find that drowned rat!"

Sean chuckled and Mickey tried, but choked, as Sean answered, "Aye'n he was washed up on the pile o' driftwood at the bend in the river, back'ere a spell," nodding to the river behind him.

"Help him up on one o' these horses and we'll go back to what's left of our camp, see if the others have found anythin'!" suggested Aiden, tossing the lead to two of the horses to his cousin.

As they rode into the trees, they heard some fussing, spitting, sloshing, and groaning and knew Patrick was probably pushing Smitty to do most of the diving for their supplies. When they came into the clearing, they reined up and leaned on the withers of the horses, watching Patrick pulling on a rope, dragging Smitty and a handful of gear from the shallow muddy water at the edge of the overflow. One wheel of the wagon showed above water, but the floodwater was still deeper than when they camped, leaving their gear and supplies, whatever remained, under water.

A tripod of stacked rifles sat in the shade of a big spruce, the same tree that had provided shelter for their fire before, but the ground had been washed free of any firewood and evidence of their temporary shelter. Closer to the tree were a pair of boxes, and one saddle, and a pile of wet blankets.

Sean, Aiden, and Mickey slipped to the ground, and the cousins took the animals to be tethered away from the water as Mickey went to the stack of gear to find a seat and catch his breath. Patrick pulled Smitty from the water, turned to look at the others and saw Mickey, "Well, where'd you come from?"

Mickey grinned, "Sean pulled me from the river where I'd washed up in some driftwood at the bend in the river. Couldn't find George," he explained, dropping his head in his hands.

When Sean and Aiden came from the trees, the others stood under the spruce except for Smitty who was busy searching for any dry wood to get a fire started. When he returned with an armful, he looked at the others, grinning and said, "We're gonna have us some coffee!"

"Coffee? How? Didn't it get washed away?" asked Sean, giving Smitty a hopeful look.

"Unnhnn, I had me a knapsack made o' that gutta percha stuff an' it's waterproof, but just to be safe, I wrapped it in one o' them waterproof ponchos we used in the war as a half tent sorta thingy, and that was the first thing I found. Watertight and dry and full o' coffee!" he declared, grinning at his companions.

"Say, 'fore we get all excited about some coffee, you might wanna know I spotted some Indians when I found the horses," stated Aiden, looking at the others who had turned their full attention to him. "There was only 'bout five or six of 'em and they was high up on the mountains on the far side of the river. So, I thought they'd not be crossin' the river too soon and figgered we was safe, but I reckoned you oughta know 'bout 'em."

"Did they see you?" asked Sean.

"Prob'ly. I think they were watchin' the horses, but like I said, they were on the far side of the river."

"Ummhmmm, and they might know of some place to cross it, too," grumbled Patrick.

"But we can't leave without gettin' the rest of our supplies, at least what we can anyway," whined Smitty, busy at building a fire.

"Well, I don't know 'bout the rest of you, but Smitty's got me hankerin' for some coffee. I think we oughta have our coffee, give it some thought, recover as much of our supplies and gear, and hightail it outta here as soon as we can!" stated Sean, looking around at the others.

Everyone seemed to agree and anxiously looked around as Smitty set the coffee pot by the fire and dug for the coffee beans and began grinding them on the close-at-hand rock. The others began checking their rifles and the ammunition they carried. Patrick suspected what the others were thinking, "We've found most of the ammunition, it's there in those two boxes and since we've all got rimfire cartridge rifles, the ammunition appears to be undamaged."

By midday, they were ready to resume their journey.

The recovered gear and supplies were loaded on the mules, and each of the men were mounted on their horses. Although they only recovered five saddles, with the loss of George Leck, they were outfitted quite well. After conferring with the treasure map and making a cursory scan of the surrounding mountains, they started upstream, heading into the canyon that Mickey had previously scouted with Leck. The trail often dipped into the edge of the river, but they made good time and by late afternoon, they had come to the fork in the river that showed a turn to the south to follow the trail that sided the smaller creek as marked on their map.

At the fork, they chose to take the shoulder on the east side and continue their journey into the deep canyon. Soon the mountains receded, giving a wider expanse to the valley and an easier trail to follow. The stream was thick with beaver ponds that often overflowed onto the trail, but the thicker black timber on the west slopes parted way for the trail and they made good time for the day. When the trail started to climb over a shoulder of the mountain, Patrick suggested they make camp in the aspen well above the creek bottom. This time, they wisely took the high ground and walked down to the water to retrieve their supply for the night.

20 / CONFRONTATION

Reuben took down the entry cover, folded it up, and put it in the pannier for the mule to pack. They finished packing up their gear and saddling the horses and with a last look around, gladly led the horses into the sunshine, mounted up and took to the trail that would take them higher up the mountain. Elly lifted her face to the warm sunshine, closed her eyes and smiled, "Ahh, that warm sunshine feels so good!"

"After that storm, and not seeing sunshine for two days, yes it does!" replied Reuben. He nodded up the trail, "There's a bit of a basin up there, but I think I'd like to take to the mountain yonder to have a good look around, maybe spot the Mouache camp."

Elly looked where he pointed, "You mean that one? The one that's above timberline?"

"Yup, reckon I can see a lot of the country from up there," he chuckled. "Looks to be a trail that goes up a ways, so, it shouldn't be too hard. You can wait for me there, in the aspen."

"Well, one thing for sure, I ain't climbin' up there!" she declared, looking at the peak that stood tall, lonely, and bald. They were on the east face of the mountain and the trail angled up the face, bent back on itself and faded into the trees that stood below a large blowdown of pines that lay like cordwood on either side of a runoff gulch that scarred the face of the mountain. It was not unusual to see such blowdowns in the high country, sometimes caused by heavy snows, other times by high winds and occasionally by fires, but there was no black on these long dead and mostly barkless trees that lay parallel with one another, and had become the habitat of marmots, badgers, and probably a few wolverines.

Reuben slid his Sharps from the scabbard, hung the binoculars around his neck, and slipped to the ground, tethering Blue to an aspen sapling and giving Elly a hand down. She could take up her sentry overlooking that vast beyond that lay behind them on the trail and fell off into the big valley to the south. Reuben grinned, saw Elly take a seat on a big rock, Bear at her feet, and he chuckled as he said, "I'll be back in a jiffy. The way that sun's warmin' the rock, you might fall asleep!"

"Now that's an idea I can warm up to," replied Elly, leaning back to stretch out on the big lichen-covered boulder. She smiled at Reuben as he started up the trail, bound for the high reaches of the mountain and his look-see.

The tall peak stood just above timberline, probably just shy of 12,000 feet and with broad shoulders that formed a ridge to the north and south. Reuben opted for the north shoulder where a faint game trail cut through the downed timber and offered an easy access. But with the altitude, nothing is easy, and Reuben was feeling the thin air as he mounted the steep slope. He stopped often for breath, his chest heaving, but he continued on and soon surmounted the shoulder and dropped to his haunches for a short rest. He scanned the countryside, kept the Sharps at his side, standing on its butt plate, to lean on. He looked due west and the row upon row of mountain peaks, some still stubbornly clinging to glaciers on the north faces of the mountains.

He sat down, took out the binoculars and began his scan. Due north, the mountains parted slightly and showed a rugged basin and a well-used trail or what could be called a wagon road that lay at the base of some steep mountains and pointed to the west, bending around a formation that was part of the range whereon he now sat. He turned to look due west down a thickly timbered cut that spread out into a wide valley and inviting basin that almost glowed green with a grassy bottom and open meadowland. He frowned, adjusted the field glasses, and propped his elbows on his knees and scanned the valley bottom. Dozens of pyramid-shaped hide tipis showed themselves, openings facing toward his promontory, and he knew he found the Mouache encampment.

He scanned the camp, guessed there to be about forty lodges, maybe more in the trees, and saw the horse herd south of the camp in the lower end of the fertile valley. It was a beautiful location in the midst of the mountains and in an area rich with game. Reuben smiled as he felt a tinge of envy, envisioning the people in the village and their peaceful lifestyle. He chuckled to himself, knowing that *peaceful* was not the right description, for they had many conflicts with settlers, gold seekers, and other native bands. It was a continual battle to keep their homes and he understood their cause.

He moved the binoculars to scan the rest of the territory, saw nothing of concern, and rose to return to Elly. As he strode into the makeshift camp, his broad smile told Elly he had some good news and she waited, smiling in return, for his report. "I found it!" he said, going to the side of Blue to return the Sharps to the scabbard. "Looks to be a good-sized village, at least forty lodges, probably a few more. Beautiful wide valley yonder. We could make it 'fore dark, if we want to, or wait till mornin' to see 'em."

Elly stood and went to her appaloosa, nodded to Reuben, "Let's just see what it takes for us to get there. We might not even make it 'fore dark."

"Alright, and we will have to take kind of a round-about way. Doesn't appear to be any trails straight down the draw, course there's prob'ly some in the trees, but I think it'll be easier just to go 'cross that saddle," nodding to the north of the basin where they were, "and go to the bottom. There's a good trail there, might even run into some settlers or…" he shrugged as he swung aboard his gelding.

With a wave of his arm, he sent Bear to scout before them and nudged Blue to follow. It was a good trail, and easy going, as it twisted through the timber, following the contours of the mountains to wend its way to the bottom where they would take the better trail south through the timber that flanked the tall mountains that lifted their granite peaks heavenward.

SEAN TOOK FIRST WATCH, FOLLOWED BY AIDEN, SMITTY, and Patrick. With two-hour shifts, that left Mickey at the first watch come daylight, which meant he also had to start the fire and begin the breakfast, most importantly get the coffee going. It was a quiet night, stars were bright, and the half-moon slowly climbed through the darkness, adding just enough light for the watchman to see the dim shadows of the trees slowly move from one side to the other. Patrick was surprised to hear the nighthawk scream in the early morning hours before dawn, but thought little of it, his mind on the landmarks detailed on the map that he had committed to memory. He walked slowly around the camp, moving from tree to tree, watching the bottom of the arroyo where the little creek trickled and gurgled down the steep mountain terrain, bouncing and splashing its way through the willows.

As the stars began to snuff their lanterns and the curtain of darkness began to give way to the encroaching pale grey of early morning, Patrick roused Mickey, whispering to him, "I laid in a fire, just got it goin', but you'll need to get the water for the coffee and start the breakfast. I'm gonna stretch out and get a few winks in 'fore we start."

Mickey grinned, sat up and stretched, lifting his rifle as he rose from his blankets. He stood, stretched again and with a big yawn, bent for the coffee pot, and started to the creek for some water. Dropping to one knee beside the little creek, he dipped the pot in the stream, waited for it to fill and stood, put the lid on the pot and turned back toward camp. He took one step, grunted as he stopped, dropped the pot, and looked at the feathered shaft protruding from his chest. He tried to speak, couldn't get his breath, and dropped to his knees, dropping his rifle and reaching toward the camp. He then fell on his face, driving the shaft through his back to protrude with the bloody flint tip pointing to the sky as he breathed his last.

The animals were tethered below the camp on the upper end of the draw, at the edge of the trees. They lifted their heads, ears pricked as they saw shadows moving through the brush and grass of the draw. The warriors were on foot, moving quickly among the low shadows of kinnikinnick, current bushes, and scrub oak. Three headed to the horses, four started for the camp, but as they neared, a rifle blasted and the leader of the band of warriors took a bullet in the chest as Patrick shouted the alarm. "Indians! Indians!"

The others were already coming from their blankets at the first shot, but now grabbed up their rifles and went to the lower edge of the camp, taking cover behind the white-barked aspen, as they began searching for targets. The dim light offered little help, the shadows of the brush and rocks were used to the advantage of the attackers, but scattered rifle fire filled the valley as one after another of the gold seekers took his shot at what he thought was an attacker. Suddenly, the horses broke from the trees, one man riding in the rear, driving the animals before him. Smitty took careful aim and fired his Henry, but the bullet was low, and the horse stumbled, throwing the rider over his head to tumble into a cluster of scrub oak. The horse struggled to his feet, took a few steps, and fell on his chest, pinning the downed rider beneath him.

As the men grew accustomed to the dim light, their bullets began to find their mark and other warriors fell beneath the barrage of rifle fire. Arrows filled the air, driving through the camp, some striking the trees, others finding purchase in gear and blankets, but one buried itself in Aiden's left shoulder, surprising the big Scot but not taking him down. Aiden looked at the shaft, grabbed it, broke it off, and lifted his rifle for another shot. The horses were milling around in the brush and grass, confused by the shooting and screaming war cries of the warriors, but when two of the warriors started for the horses, they were dropped by the bullets from the men in the trees.

The leader of the attackers, a young warrior, shouted to the others in a language not understood by the white men, and the warriors sifted through the brush and disappeared. They had taken enough losses; it would be foolish and too costly to lose any more warriors in such a fight. Even though the prize would be the horses, there were not enough horses to risk the lives of any more warriors.

When the gold seekers realized the Indians had left, they came from the trees to round up the horses. It was Sean that discovered the body of Mickey and he hollered to the others, "Hey! Mickey's down!" Aiden and Smitty had caught up the animals and only Patrick came to Sean's side. They stood, looking at the body of their friend, "After surviving the flood, and now this," said Sean, shaking his head and reaching down to lift the body. "We'll bury him near the camp, then get on our way 'fore they come back," he declared without waiting for the others. As he turned, Mickey's body in arms, he saw the bloody chest of his cousin. He stopped and stared at the man, who chuckled and answered his unspoken question, "Yeah, I took one. You can take it out when we get back to camp."

Smitty led the mules into the camp, looked at the others and said, "We lost a horse, that black mare. And there's a Injun pinned underneath his body, still alive."

Sean and Patrick looked up at Smitty, frowning, and Sean said, "What'd you do?"

"Nuthin'. Thought I'd see what you all wanted to do. We could leave him be, kill 'im, or pull him out and use him, maybe as a guide or sumpin'."

Patrick frowned, looked from Smitty to Sean and Aiden. He thought a moment, then said to Sean, "Let's go see," and started to the downed animal. Sean was close behind and drew up beside him as they looked at the young warrior, his legs underneath the horse and the young man looked with hatred at the two men. He snarled his lip and spat words of contempt and daring at the white men. Although neither could understand what he said, they knew what he meant.

Sean asked, "Can you speak English?"

The young warrior snarled and growled again, said something else, but it was not in English, and the men looked at one another. Sean shrugged, and moved closer, looked back at Patrick, and said, "Let's see if we can get him out. I'll push and lift on the horse, you pull on him." He nodded toward the young man.

Patrick waited till Sean was in place, then walked up behind the warrior, grabbed him under the armpits and as Sean put his back to the horse and pushed with his legs, pulling and lifting at the mane and shoulder of the horse, they pulled the young man free. He tried to scramble to his feet, winced at the pain, and they saw his lower left leg was broken and bent at an angle away from the other. The young man stared at the leg, looked up at the men and back at the leg. He was frightened and in pain but did not know what to do or what they were going to do, and he sat still, hands on the ground beside his hips as he tried to tolerate the pain, but it showed on his face and Sean knew he was hurting.

Sean looked at Patrick, "See if you can fetch me some sticks to use as a splint," and turned to see Smitty coming near. He hollered, "Fetch me something for bandages. Boy's got a broken leg!"

They were down another man, but with the young

warrior now bound to the horse, they were mounted on the five remaining horses and leading the pack mules. It was about mid-morning when they were back on the trail, after burying Mickey and gathering up the horses and mending Aiden and the young warrior. But they traveled silently. They started with six, now there were four, and they were no nearer their treasure than before, or at least it seemed that way, although they gained one with the native and hoped he would be of help to guide them. But so far, their communication was limited to crude sign language. Hopeful for something better, each man was intent on his own thoughts, each one counting their own cost and the slim possibility of riches, a possibility that was becoming smaller and more remote, but they moved on, for there was nothing else that mattered now. The price had been high, but little did they know it would probably be higher still before they could leave these mountains.

21 / UTE

The sun was off their right shoulder as they rode from the trees into the wide-open grassy valley. It had been a challenging ride, following the trail that sided Wolf Creek as it came from the mountains was the easy part. The last half-mile, when it dropped off the steep shoulder and the creek cascaded over the rocks, was little more than an eyebrow shelf first on the north side, then crossed the little creek to hang on the south side around the bluff and duck back into the trees. Reuben drew to a stop just as they came from the trees and leaned on the pommel to look around at the park that held the village. Although the near side was dotted with tall spruce, fir, and pines, some stretching as tall as sixty and seventy feet. Aspen were plentiful, showing the light green of new leaves that fluttered in the wind, and the undergrowth added the rusty color of oak brush. Belly-deep grass waved in the easy breeze as if beckoning the visitors onward, and with a broad smile to Elly and a slight nod, Reuben bumped the ribs of his blue roan with his heels and started toward the village.

The valley was framed by granite peaks, limestone

cliffs, and basaltic rimrock that jutted from the deep green of the pine forest sprinkled with the pale green of aspen. The cotton ball white clouds danced across the azure blue sky and wherever they looked, they were filled with awe at the beauty of the Creator. As the horses walked through the line of spruce, Blue lifted his head and paused, looking across the park at five riders coming at a canter toward them. Reuben spoke to Elly, "Here they come, easy now. Keep your hands in sight," as he watched the approach of the warriors.

As they neared, they brandished their weapons, lances, bows with arrows nocked, and two had rifles, both older muskets. One man came to the front of the others, shouting his demands in the Shoshonean tongue of the people, but Reuben dropped his looped reins on the neck of Blue and lifted his hands, using sign language, as he spoke, "We come in peace. We come to see our friend, Kaniache. We are Reuben and Elly, or Man with the Blue Horse, and Yellow Bird," as he nodded to Elly. "We lived near your people in the valley of the Sangre de Cristo, two summers past."

The warriors spoke among themselves, gesturing to the intruders, but the leader who said his name was Yellow Nose, knew of these people. He turned back to Reuben and Elly and spoke in English, "You come," and swung his horse around, looked over his shoulder at them, frowned at Bear who stood beside Blue's front leg, and started back to the village. They splashed across the shallows of Wolf Creek and came into the grassy flat with the village. The warriors rode before and behind the two visitors and led the group into the village. Several of the women and many children came near to look at the newcomers, the children reacting to the big dog and Bear responding with a wagging tail and soft eyes.

As they neared the center of the village, several women came closer, and one spoke as she reached up to Reuben, "Reuben! You saved me and others from the Comanche! I am White Crane!" She looked around and motioned to another, "And here is Little Turtle! We were both taken by the Comanche, but you came after us! Because of you, we are with our people!" The two women walked alongside, White Crane keeping her hand on the shoulder of Blue and talking to the others, obviously telling them about Reuben's rescue.

The warriors stopped in front of the leader's lodge and slipped to the ground. The warrior, Yellow Nose, that had spoken before, motioned to Reuben and Elly to dismount and turned to face the village leader as he came from the lodge. An impressive figure, broad shouldered, deep chested and with a stoic expression, he stood as he exited the tipi, scowling at the leader of the warriors and glancing at Reuben and Elly. He grunted at the man who began to explain, motioning toward the couple and back to the chief.

Kaniache turned to face Reuben and nodded, stepped closer, and extended his arm. "Máykh!"

Reuben nodded and reached out to grasp forearms with the chief and spoke, "Máykh! Greetings Kaniache! It has been a long time since last we met." He turned slightly to motion to Elly to come forward, "You remember my woman, Elly, or Yellow Bird."

The chief nodded with nothing more than a glance to Elly, and turned back to Reuben, but his attention was taken by the two women who stepped forward. White Crane began chattering about the time they were taken by the Comanche and how Reuben came to their rescue and how Elly also helped them. Although she spoke in the tongue of the people, she finished her talk with, "They are great friends of the Ute People," declared White Crane in English, smiling, and nodding at the two visitors.

"Why do you come among our people," asked Kaniache, frowning at Reuben, maintaining his stoic expression and the dignity of a chief.

"We are friends of you and your people. We lived in the valley beyond the Sangre de Cristos with the Jicarilla and the Mouache. We would like to visit and if you are interested, we would also talk with you of peace with the white people. I am a marshal for the territory, and part of my duty is to keep peace among the whites, and between the whites and the great Mouache."

Kaniache looked sternly at Reuben and turned to Elly. He glanced to White Crane and spoke in their tongue to tell her to take the visitors to the empty lodge and prepare them a meal. He looked back to Reuben, "After you have had your meal, I will come to your fire, and we will talk." Without waiting for a response, he turned away and disappeared into his tipi.

Reuben glanced to Elly, but White Crane spoke to her, "You will come with me. I will show you to your lodge and we will prepare a meal for you." She smiled as she led the pair, looked at them and said, "It is a great honor for our chief to come to you. It is not often done."

Elly smiled, glanced to Reuben, and replied to White Crane, "We would enjoy a meal with you and your people. Thank you."

The lodge was closer to the tree line and about fifty yards from the central compound before the lodge of the chief. White Crane flipped aside the hide hanging over the entry and motioned to the lodge, but quickly turned away to go with Little Turtle for the makings for the meal. Reuben began stripping the animals, stacking their gear within the lodge, and stepped out to give the animals a rubdown but was surprised to see two young men readying to lead the horses and mule away. "Whoa, wait on there!" he declared, but a voice from behind him said, "They will tend to your animals," and Reuben turned to see White Crane, already busy preparing the cook fire. "They will do a good job of caring for them and make sure they get water and graze."

"Oh, well, alright then," he answered. He started to turn away, but White Crane motioned to a pair of willow backrests near the entry to the tipi. With a nod, he dropped to the blanket, and seated himself to take advantage of the backrest. He locked his fingers behind his head and smiled as Elly came from the lodge.

She looked at him, shaking her head, "Don't get too comfortable, I might volunteer you to wash dishes!" she giggled.

"You know that ain't about to happen," grumbled Reuben, not that he was averse to helping his woman, but among the native people, that was strictly women's work and men were to tend to important things, like hunting, fighting, making weapons, and in general, being waited on by the women. He leaned back, smiling, "I could get used to this!"

"Hah!" declared Elly, shaking her head as she walked to the other women.

SHORTLY AFTER THEY FINISHED THEIR MEAL, KANIACHE and his woman walked into the light of the fire and Kaniache joined Reuben beside the fire, enjoying the comfortable backrests. They spoke for a short while before Reuben asked, "So, what do you think about peace with the white man? Ouray is going to help draw up a new treaty, he's camped at Fort Garland even now."

Kaniache growled, "Ouray does not speak for my people! He has already given away too much of our land. Before the white man came, our people would go every year at greenup, into the plains beyond the mountains," motioning with a broad swoop of his arm, "and have our buffalo hunt, and again at the time of colors. But now, there are white men and their wagons. They make mud huts and ruin the land with their plows and animals and kill the buffalo and leave them to rot in the sun! They have no respect for what the Creator gave to our people! They dig in the dirt for their yellow stones, leave their filth and trash behind and the Creator weeps at the way they ruin His creation!"

"You speak of the Creator, what is it that you know of the Creator?" asked Reuben.

Kaniache frowned, looking at Reuben with a glare that showed incredulity, and asked, "Do you not know the Creator?"

"Yes, I do. But how do you know and what do you know about Him?"

"I learned of him from the black robes and from those who call themselves missionaries. But we called the Creator Sinawav in our creation stories. It is told that in the beginning Sinawav was with coyote and gave coyote a bag to take to the sacred land, but he was not to open the bag. When coyote left and was out of sight of Sinawav, he stopped and opened the bag and many of the little creatures jumped out and scattered, but coyote closed the bag while there were still others inside. He went to the sacred valley and dumped them out there.

When he returned and told Sinawav what happened, Sinawav said, 'You are foolish and have done a fearful thing. Those that were left, were the Ute people. But those that escaped, will fight with our people forever."

"Then what do you believe about the hereafter, you know, about what happens when you die?"

Kaniache frowned, "We will go to what the white man calls Heaven and be with the Creator, Sinawav."

"And what do you believe about the white man?"

"They will all go to hell!"

Reuben chuckled, dropped his eyes, and shook his head slightly, "Then let's talk about peace for now."

"It is good. You said you were to keep peace between the white man and the natives, yet they still come into our land. This," he motioned to the land around them, "has always been the land of the Mouache or Moghwachi Núuchi, the Kapuuta Núuchi, Tavi'wachi Núuchi, and Wʉgama Núuchi." He held up all fingers of both hands, "This many summers ago, our chief Cany Attle told the white men, the valley of the big river, what the white man calls San Luis Valley, was the land of the Núuchi people. But Ouray of the Tavi'wachi Núuchi, made a treaty to give all that land to the white man, but no other chiefs agreed!

"Every time the white man makes a treaty, our people give away our land on the promises of the white man. They took Ouray and others to the land of the great white father and made more promises, but the white man's promises are as the dust in the air, nothing comes of them!" He spat, grabbed a handful of dirt, and let it sift through his fingers and glared at Reuben. "Now, you want to take more land and make more promises? I say no! We helped Carson in the fight with the Navajo, we captured many sheep and horses, but he took most of them, just like the empty promises he gives. I will lead the Moghwachi Núuchi to reclaim the land of our people! It is our land; we will drive out the white man and take our land back!

"White man says no one will come into our land to take the yellow stone, or to build their mud huts, but still they come. There are others even now that have come into our land to look for the gold. My warriors have been watching them and they come, but they will be stopped! My son, Running Elk, is with the warriors that watch the white man, and they will not come further into our land! Did you not say it is your duty to keep them out?"

"Yes, and when I leave here, I will go to them and make them leave. I thought the storm that just passed would drive them away, but if it did not, I will make them leave."

Kaniache looked at Reuben, judging his intent, and slowly nodded. "You have been a friend of my people. It is good that you will do this. Maybe then, we can talk more of peace." With another stern look at Reuben, Kaniache rose to his feet, motioned to his woman to come, and the two walked from the light of the cookfire.

22 / COERCION

Walking hand in hand, Reuben and Elly made their way through the village toward the central compound to visit with Kaniache a bit more regarding his peace efforts. "Do you think he'll be open to the idea of peace with the whites?" asked Elly.

"Kaniache is a smart man, and his concern is for his people. But he wants to reclaim the land given away by Ouray in that last treaty. Like he said, all this land was theirs," he motioned with a wide sweep of his arm, "and that includes the San Luis Valley and the plains to the east where the Arapaho, Cheyenne, and Kiowa are fighting with the white man. But I think he'd be happy if he could reclaim the San Luis Valley, it'd be a victory for him and his people. Buffalo come into the valley, not like they do in the plains, but at least there are some. Can't say as I blame 'em none, they've got a bum deal. All because of a bunch of gold-hungry prospectors and settlers!"

The peaceful morning was shattered by a band of warriors riding into the village, yelling and wailing, their horses kicking up dust and more as they slid to a stop before the lodge of Kaniache. Two horses carried the bodies of two warriors and the other warriors slipped to the ground to stand before Kaniache as he came from his lodge.

"Kaniache! Your son, Running Elk, and three others have been killed by the white men that came into our land! We fought, killed one, and bloodied others, but still they live and come!"

White Crane came to the side of Reuben and Elly, quietly translating the words of the returning warriors. When the leader of the party, Spotted Crow, told of the killing of Kaniache's son, she stopped with her hand to her mouth, and struggled to continue.

Kaniache's eyes flared, and his jaw tightened as he listened to the report, "How many white men?" he demanded, glowering at the warrior before him.

"There are at least four, maybe more. They have many guns that shoot many times!"

It is often the way of a man that fails in his task or duty to find any reason or justification for that failure and Spotted Crow pleaded when he spoke of the guns of the white men. Kaniache's eyes burned with anger and sorrow at the thought of his son being killed by the intruders to their land. His thoughts churned, remembering the many words about treaties. Even this land that had been promised by the last treaty, to be theirs forever and white men would not be allowed to enter, and yet they come.

Kaniache walked to the horses with the bodies, lifted each face to look at the dead man, growling and grumbling with each step. He turned, glaring at the others, and shouted, "We go to rid the land of the white man! We go to get my son!" He glanced at Reuben, his eyes blazing and his nostrils flaring, motioned to the bodies of the warriors, "This is the work of your people! This is what your treaties do!"

Reuben stepped closer, "Kaniache, my heart is heavy for the loss of your son, but more death and blood will not help. Let us go before you, it is my job to take these men back to the fort so they can be punished, and I will do that. But if you kill them, the soldiers will come, and many will die!"

"It is my right to get my son! If the white men are there, I will kill them!"

The other warriors were still there, watching and listening to Kaniache. Reuben turned to the leader, "Did the white men attack you, or did you attack them?"

Spotted Crow listened as White Crane translated, and growled, "We went after their horses! They had many horses!"

"So, you were trying to steal their horses and they shot at you?"

"Yes! We killed one who was alone at the water so we could go for the horses, then they shot at us, and we returned fire!"

Reuben looked at Kaniache, "If someone was stealing your horses, wouldn't you try to stop them, shoot them?"

Kaniache did not answer, just clenched his jaw, and looked from Reuben to Spotted Crow and back.

Reuben stepped closer to Kaniache and with a lowered voice, "Kaniache, let me and my woman go first, let Spotted Crow lead me back to the camp of the white men. If I cannot get them to go with me back to Fort Garland for their punishment, then you can have them. Just give me that chance. You don't want any more of your men killed by these men that are anxious to kill more of your people, just let me go first."

Kaniache lifted his chin, glared at Reuben through

squinted eyes, and turned quickly to the other warriors, "Black Wolf, go with Reuben and Yellow Bird. Take them to the place of these white men!" He turned back to Reuben, "Black Wolf can speak your tongue. You will have two fingers of time with these men, then we will destroy them!"

"THAT! THAT RIGHT THERE! THAT'S A WATERFALL! YOU know, where the water from the stream comes down a great distance and splashes into a big pool!" stated Patrick, motioning to the emblem on the map and trying to make himself understood by moving about, motioning with his hands to the stream, lifting them high and pantomiming the water falling and splashing. He was almost shouting as his frustration increased, trying to make the young warrior understand. It is common for those that believe others cannot understand, they try to raise the volume of their voice as if making the words louder make them more easily understood, but the problem is not with the hearing, it's with the understanding.

Patrick paced around, shaking his head, and returned to the map that lay on the big flat rock. Running Elk sat on the edge of the rock, looking at the map and watching the antics of the crazy white man. He shook his head slightly, wondering if all white men were crazy like this one. Patrick returned to the map, pointed again at the waterfall, then traced the squiggly line that indicated the stream and spoke slowly, "This is the stream, water," pointing at the stream below the camp, "When the water comes from high," he pointed up the mountain and mimicked the water flowing down, "and it gets steep, it becomes a waterfall." He made the sounds of water running, then motioned like it went over a steep embankment and made motions like it falling a long ways, then made the crashing and roaring sound of the water hitting the pool at the bottom. Running Elk slowly let a bit of a grin show, and began nodding his head, pointing at the map. Patrick got excited, "You know? You understand? Waterfall?" making the motions again and returned to the map, pointing at the drawing. Running Elk spoke in his own language, "The fall of water, high," motioning high by looking up and pointing, then made the motion of water falling and made the noise, then pointed at the map. He grinned broadly and pointed through the cut where the trail split the mountains, and said, "One day!" and with arms held before him, one on top of the other and crossed before his chest, he brought the upper hand, held stiff with the arm, up high, and made the motion of the sun rising and crossing the sky and setting.

Patrick got excited, turned to the others, and said, "He understands! He says the waterfall is one day, the rise of the sun and the setting, that's one day! We're gettin' close, boys! We're gettin' close!"

"Then let's be done with eatin' and get to packin'!" declared Smitty, excitement showing on his whiskery face. The others nodded and made short work of their breakfast and as Patrick began cleaning up the camp, the Scotsmen led the horses and mules into the clearing and began rigging the animals, with Smitty lending a hand.

It was mid-morning when they finally got on the trail, but the excitement gave them a renewed energy and their thoughts were on the treasure and possible riches. They had but rounded the point of the ridge above their camp when they broke into the open, overlooking a grassy park that lay at the bottom of a long granite-tipped ridge with a bit of icy cornice hanging below the edge of the ridge. Patrick frowned as he looked at the rocky formation, reined up, and pulled out the map. He looked at the drawing, up at the ridge, and back at the map. He grinned broadly, turned to the men, "That's the ridge before the mountain! We're gettin' close! It should be just beyond that ridge!" he pointed excitedly, twisting around in his seat to look at the others. He turned back to look at the trail and back at the map, "See here! The trail goes around that ridge and the mountain is just on the other side!"

He frowned, looked closer at the map, and looked at the men that had come alongside, "We need to watch for that fleur-de-lis. I don't know if it'll be carved on the rocks, maybe a tree, or something else."

"Don't that mean lily flower?" asked Smitty, lifting the edge of his hat to scratch at the almost bald dome, as he looked around.

"That's what it means, but…" shrugged Patrick, looking about them.

"Is it before or after the waterfall?" asked Sean.

"Beside it, so it could be on the cliff, a tree, or something else."

"So, there's no sense looking for it till we find the waterfall, right?"

"Yeah, I s'pose, unless the creek moved cuz of a storm, or somethin', then the fleur-de-lis would be where it was originally, so, just in case, let's keep lookin' as we work our way to the waterfall the Indian says he knows."

Patrick put the map back in the leather tube, stuffed it inside his jacket, and lifted the reins as he nudged his mount forward. He was in the lead, the Indian directly behind him, hands bound together, and the others followed, trailing the pack mules, all anxious to find the waterfall and the sign that would guide them to the lost treasure. With thoughts about the treasure filling their minds and their eyes searching only for clues, no one noticed the riders that were coming toward them, a few miles further down the trail.

23 / CONFLICT

Patrick took the lead as the trail angled up the high mountain, cutting through the black timber. As they rounded the shoulder of the mountain, the trail had been obliterated by a mudslide that came down a natural avalanche chute and filled the creek bottom with timber, boulders, and mud. He stepped down and walked closer, looking across the debris and rocks, turned to the men, "I think we can make it across, but I'm gonna try and walk it, leadin' my horse. Wait until I get across and I'll wave you over."

The cousins and the Indian had crowded together when Patrick stopped, and now Sean nodded, "Take it easy, it don't look none too stable!" As he spoke, he looked high and low for another crossing, but nothing showed, and he looked down as Patrick mounted the edge of the slide and started across.

It took some finagling, stumbling, kicking, and tossing of branches and rocks, but Patrick made it across and once over, hollered back, "You can make it, just watch your step!" and stood as the others started to cross. With the pack mules' leads tied to the tails of the horses, each man started across on foot, leading his animals behind. When the last man, Smitty, crossed, they had made a passable trail that would probably be used by many others. Once across, they mounted up and resumed their trek.

The trail made a wide bend around the big talus slope, continued westerly and held to the shoulder of the mountains on the north side. They cut through a notch and the trail, now siding the headwaters of Wolf Creek, bent to the west southwest, and wound through the thick spruce and fir of the high country. A wide park showed through the trees, south of the trail, and revealed a saddle between the long ridge and the mountain peak that Patrick assumed was the mountain that held the treasure. A break in the thicker trees caused them to pause, step down, and look at the park and the mountain that showed a peak that stood just a few hundred feet above timberline.

Patrick looked at the others, grinning, "I'm thinkin' that's the mountain with the treasure. But we gotta find that waterfall, maybe the fleur-de-lis, for the starting point to get us to the exact location. That's where he'll" nodding to the Indian who sat stoically on his mount, "come in and show us where it is. The way he acted, that waterfall ain't too far. So, let's get mounted and keep goin'!"

The trail dropped from the trees, pointed to a slight rise and wide saddle. As they crested the saddle, Sean reined up and spoke just loud enough for Patrick to hear, "Riders! Looks like three of 'em!" and pointed to the winding trail that sided a bald slope about a mile away.

Patrick looked where Sean pointed, stood in his stirrups, and stared in the distance. He twisted around and looked to Sean and the others, "I can't tell if they're Injuns or not. Looks like they got a pack mule, but…"

"What would white men be doin' 'round here?" asked Smitty.

"Same thing we're doin', lookin' for gold!" answered Aiden, shaking his head.

"Smitty, you cut through the timber yonder," pointing to the trees on the far side of the creek, "see if you can get behind 'em. Sean, try to find a spot in the trees there, on the uphill side. You can leave your mule with Aiden." He looked to Aiden, "You and me, we'll stay here in the trail till we can see who and what they are, and if they're Injuns, we'll cut loose on 'em right quick!"

Black Wolf rode beside Reuben, to his left, with his Springfield rifle across the withers of his mount. Reuben frowned when he recognized the rifle as one of the common .58 caliber rifles of the war, used by both Union and Confederate forces. He looked to Black Wolf, "Did you trade for that rifle?" nodding to the weapon.

"Yes, from a soldier in grey."

Reuben looked up the trail, "How much further?"

Black Wolf pointed ahead, "There, trail goes around point, then between mountains."

Reuben stood in his stirrups, looking to the east and with a glance to the sun high overhead, he frowned and leaned forward slightly, settled back in his seat, and spoke just loud enough for Elly, who had drawn closer, to hear. "I think they're layin' an ambush. Thought I saw one below the trail, and if so, there's prob'ly one high. We'll keep goin' but slip your rifle outta the scabbard and keep it handy." As he spoke, he casually slipped the

Henry from the scabbard and lay it across the pommel of his saddle. With a nod, he nudged Blue to walk forward. Black Wolf did the same, but lowered his rifle to his side, ready to fire the weapon one-handed, pistol-style.

As they neared the edge of the thicker trees, Reuben could make out a man, sitting astraddle his mount, waiting in the middle of the trail. He thought he could see another, maybe beside and slightly behind. When within about forty yards, the man in the trees hailed them, "Stop where you are!"

Reuben halted, causing both Black Wolf and Elly to stop. Reuben lifted one hand high, "Sounds like you're a white man, am I right?" responded Reuben. "Come outta those trees where we can see you and we can talk!" The man slowly came from the shadows, other movement behind him, and two other riders showed, but movement suggested more animals and probably more men. As they came into the open, Black Wolf said in a low voice, "That is Running Elk! The son of Kaniache!"

Bear was to Reuben's right, near the roan's leg and let a low growl rumble. Reuben spoke softly, "Easy Bear." With his hand still held high he continued, "I'm Deputy Marshal Reuben Grundy," and with a slight nod added, "and this is my friend, Black Wolf, and the one behind..." But before he could finish, a rifle blasted from the trees, startling the horses, making them jump slightly, making the riders jerk tight on the reins. Black Wolf moaned, grabbed at his chest, and slumped over the neck of his horse. Before the echo of the first shot returned, another rifle blasted from the trees below and behind them.

Reuben had swung his Henry around, earing back the hammer in the same movement and fired toward the men in the trees who were frantically backing their horses into the trees. The speaker jerked to the side, swung his mount around and shouldered the horse with Running Elk aboard and took off on the trail through the shadow-mottled trees. Reuben was the only one who fired his rifle and with no other targets within sight, he twisted around to see Black Wolf loosen his grip on the mane of his horse and slide to the ground. But a moan from behind made him quickly turn to see Elly who had also fallen to the ground. Bear had run to her side and was now beside the appaloosa, licking the face of the woman, who did not stir.

Reuben instantly hit the ground and ran to Elly's side, his Henry still gripped tightly. He glanced at Elly, made a quick scan of the trees round about, and dropped to the ground beside her. Laying his rifle aside, he began moving Elly to her back, looking for where she had been hit. He saw blood high on her left side, a torn hole in her tunic and he quickly stripped away the tunic, saw the wound where the bullet had ripped away her flesh in a long gouge, blood flowing from the long tear, and he looked at her face. Her eyes were closed, her breathing ragged, and he looked and felt all over, searching for any other wound. When he brought his hand from behind her head, there was blood and he had felt the beginning of a knot.

Carefully lifting her head, he looked at the injury, saw it was a small gash, probably from the fall. He thought that was probably what knocked her out, and gently lay her head down. He began to examine the deeper wound under her arm where the bullet had torn the flesh, exposing a bit of a rib, and he looked around, saw the unmoving form of Black Wolf and the horses standing, reins trailing, but there was no sign of the attackers. He went to the pack mule, grabbed the parfleche that was

Elly's medicine kit and a couple of blankets and returned to her side.

He made a bit of a bed at the side of the trail where the grass was deep for cushion, and with one blanket doubled and stretched out, he lifted Elly and lay her gently on the blanket and covered her with the other. He looked at the wound again and began washing it clean with the water from the water bag. Once he was satisfied, he looked again, shook his head, and dug in the kit for a curved needle and some linen thread. The wound was bleeding, but not heavily. Reuben daubed at it, looking at the source of the blood, concerned he might have to cauterize the wound before sewing, but decided it would not be necessary and began sewing the long gouge.

When he finished, he cleaned the area around the wound and began to bandage. He scooped up a ball of ointment from Elly's special potion of the Balm of Gilead made from the sap of fresh buds of the aspen tree, some sage leaves, and osha root ground into a salve, and smeared it on the bandage of the folded linen patch. He applied some of the salve directly to the wound, then the compress with more of the salve, and began wrapping the bandage and linen strips to make the bandage secure. Once the bandaging was finished, he retrieved her fresh tunic from the bedroll and replaced the torn and bloody one. Satisfied he had done all he could for her, he looked around and realized there was more to be done. They needed a better campsite, near the water, and room for the horses. He also had to tend to the body of Black Wolf.

He spotted a small clearing in the trees below the trail and near the little creek and began moving everything there to set up camp. He was just settling in when he glanced to the trail and spotted the approach of the war party led by Kaniache. As they neared, he stepped from the trees and stopped Kaniache.

"What happened?" growled the chief.

"We were ambushed. Black Wolf was killed," he turned to point to the camp. "His body is there, near the horses," he turned back to face Kaniache, "but before he was killed, he saw your son, Running Elk, held as a captive of the gold seekers." He paused, looking at the chief and his reaction, but seeing only a frown on the chief, he continued. "My woman was also wounded."

Kaniache glared at Reuben, turned to look toward the camp, "Will she live?"

"Yes, I have bandaged the wound, but she can't ride now. We will stay here."

"Where are the white men?" demanded Kaniache.

"They took off back up the trail," he pointed toward the trail and looked back at the chief. "Kaniache, if you can take them alive, I will still take them to the fort for punishment. It would be best to do it that way. Now that your son lives, maybe you can get them to surrender."

The chief glared at Reuben, his lip snarling in contempt, "They will pay for taking my son. If my son dies, they will take a long time to die, and my people will watch them die!" he declared, and Reuben knew what Kaniache meant when he said they would die slow. The native people have many ways of making a captive enemy suffer, each tribe perfecting their own way of torturing a man and often letting the women have their way to find retribution for the sins of the enemy. It would not be an easy death for them. Yet Reuben knew there was nothing he could do to dissuade the Ute chief, and he was not sure he would want to, after all, those men had tried to kill his wife.

24 / CHASE

"There!" shouted Patrick, gesturing to the faint trail that pointed to the saddle between the long ridge and the low peak. He had already rallied the others when he shouted and took to the trees at the ambush. He did not want to face the marshal and the thoughts of prison and lost gold ran through his mind as he slapped legs to his mount, pulling tight on the lead of the horse that carried Running Elk.

It was a rough trail that wound through the trees, cutting back on itself to mount the steep hillside, a hill-side scarred by the deep cut from the spring runoff. The horses dug deep, humping their backs as they lunged up the mountainside, the riders laying low on the necks of the animals, fearful of being caught by the small group they attacked. The game trail broke into the open as it neared the arroyo and Patrick reined up, letting the horses have a breather and giving the others time to catch up to the leader.

He stepped down and stood, sides heaving, and bent with hands on knees as he sucked wind, trying to fill his lungs with the thin mountain air. He stood, looking down the trail to see the last of their number, the wiry one known as Smitty, slapping legs to his mount, calling the black gelding every name he could think of and adding a few originals. When he drew near, he looked at the others, twisted in his saddle to look at their back trail, and dropped to the ground beside Aiden.

Patrick glared at the others, stared at Smitty, "I told you not to shoot unless we opened the ball!"

Smitty stood and with a snarl, "I didn't start it! He did!" pointing at Sean.

"That Injun was liftin' his rifle, gettin' ready to shoot! I had to put him down!" responded the big Scotsman, looking from Patrick to his cousin, Aiden.

"Then why'd *you* shoot?" growled Patrick, turning to look at the whiskery face of the older man.

"At first, I din't know it was him," nodding to Sean, "an' I thought you had done the shootin' and we was to take 'em all out."

"Didn't you hear him say he was a deputy marshal?" growled Patrick, looking from Smitty to Sean.

"A marshal?" repeated Sean, glancing to his cousin to see him slowly nod.

"And the other'n was a woman!" added Patrick, shaking his head at their predicament.

"My father will come soon!" stated Running Elk, the first time he had spoken English before the men.

Patrick turned to the Indian, "So, now you can talk huh?"

"My father, Kaniache, is the chief of our people. He will come soon," he turned to look back at the trail. From their vantage, the trail that sided Wolf Creek could be seen as it came from the thicker timber, about where the attack had occurred.

"So, now we have the whole tribe of Indians after us,

and with you shootin' the woman, we have the marshal after us, the only ones missin' is the army!" declared Aiden, shaking his head as he looked from Sean to Smitty.

Smitty dropped his eyes, shook his head, and mumbled, "With our luck, they're already on our trail!"

Patrick flared, "Ain't nobody gonna keep us from that gold! We're too close now to give up on it or let anybody or anything keep us from it!" He turned away from the others, grabbed up the rein of his mount and stepped in the stirrup but was stopped when Sean said, "Hey! You're bleedin'! Did you take a bullet?"

Patrick let out a deep breath, shook his head as he stood with one foot in the stirrup, the other still on the ground. He dropped his head to the saddle and slowly turned around, slipping his foot from the stirrup, and stood to face the men. "Yeah, I took a bullet, an' it's still in there!" nodding to his right shoulder, "But we ain't got time to do nothin' with it now. We gotta put some distance between us an' them Injuns!" pointing to the trail below the rise. They could see several riders dropping from the trail, taking to the draw below, about a mile behind them.

The others turned to look and glanced back to Patrick who had mounted up and started his mount down the trail into the arroyo, dragging the horse and captive behind. Sean glanced to Aiden and Smitty, "He's got the map!" and mounted up to follow Patrick.

Kaniache looked from Reuben to the unconscious Elly and back, swung aboard his horse, saw a warrior coming from the trees and held up his hand to stop the others. The lone warrior came to Kaniache, reported in their tongue and Kaniache nodded, looked at Reuben, "The white men have taken the trail over the rise between the ridge and peak," he pointed to the high rising mountain behind Reuben, "where the creeks are divided. That leads to the bottom and the East Fork of the San Juan River. That river comes from the mountains at the low end of the park where our village lies. If they go there, they will meet other warriors of my people!" He spoke to the man immediately behind him and with a nod the warrior turned his mount and took off back down the trail to their village, kicking his mount up to a canter. Kaniache nodded to Reuben and started up the draw to take the trail over the saddle crossing.

"Reuben?" the call was little more than a whisper, but he quickly turned and went to Elly's side. She was struggling to keep her eyes open and lifted a hand toward him, "What happened?"

"It was an ambush. You were wounded, a deep graze on your side, deep enough to expose a rib, and you fell and hit a rock or something that knocked you out, split your scalp a mite and you've prob'ly got a good-sized goose egg! But other'n that, you're fine as ever!" He smiled as he sat beside her, lifting her hand in his and resting it on his leg.

Elly frowned, winced as she tried to move, felt the back of her head, and scowled, "Oww, that *is* a big knot!"

"That ain't nothin'. I had to sew up your side there. You're lucky you were unconscious when I did, cuz, well, it ain't as purty as you'd make it, but it'll do!"

"What about those men?"

"They took outta here lickety-split, but I think I put some lead into one of 'em."

"Did I hear you tell them you were a deputy?"

"I did, but the ones in the trees did the shootin' and they might not have heard it."

"We goin' after 'em?"

"No, and there probably won't be much left of 'em after Kaniache catches up with 'em."

Elly frowned, looking around, dropped her hand to Bear's head who had scooted closer to her. "So, Kaniache's bound to get his revenge for the killing of his son, is he?"

"His son wasn't killed. The gold hunters had him as a captive. Black Wolf saw him behind the leader of the bunch, told me it was Running Elk right before they opened fire on us. Black Wolf was killed, but I told Kaniache his son was alive. He didn't take it quite like I expected, he was even madder, if that's possible. Just made him more determined to catch up to 'em. He said if they killed his son, they would die a slow death!" Reuben chuckled.

"That's not good," frowned Elly, looking at Reuben.

"To tell you the truth, I was ready to kill 'em myself when I saw you down on the ground, and you were still unconscious when Kaniache stopped so I didn't try to talk him out of his revenge. I was none too happy with 'em, still ain't!"

"I think I can ride, so we should go after them," began Elly, trying to sit up but wincing and grabbing at her side.

"We're not going anywhere. You try ridin' with that and you'll split it open again and just make it worse. I bandaged it with your special salve and such, so you should be alright, but we'll take it easy right here for a day or two. Then we'll see what we need to do, maybe just go back to the fort, and rest up a mite."

"I'm hungry," said Elly, smiling at her man.

"I take it that's your hint for me to go find us some fresh meat?"

With another smile and a nod, "But how 'bout a fire first?"

He was gone but a short while and as he walked back into their camp, he was grinning and held up a fat turkey for Elly to feast her eyes on their supper. He wasted little time plucking and cleaning the bird, soon had it on a spit over the fire and the coffee pot was dancing. Before putting the coffee in the pot, he used some of the water to make a tea from the inner bark of the willows and let Elly sip on the hot brew. He buried some yampa roots to bake and sat back to watch the meal cook. Elly had fallen asleep and had a slight smile showing, apparently experiencing a little relief from the pain by sipping the tea. Reuben smiled, leaned back, content for the moment, but his thoughts turned to the gold seekers, and he wondered how the chase was going, certain that Kaniache would overtake the pilgrims before too long. He shook his head as he thought of what they would face, knowing there would be little mercy with the chief.

25 / KANIACHE

The horses were winded and stumbling when Patrick begrudgingly reined up and stepped down, looking back at the others as they struggled up the steeper hillside, every horse lathered and winded, heads hanging and the froth of lather at their mouths. When the animals stopped, the men slid to the ground and looked at their backtrail. With the timber on the north face, a mix of standing dead snags and thin fir and lodgepole pine, they could see into the woods and about a half-mile of the trail in the areas of thin timber. Most of the men had dropped to their haunches or sat on the rocks, loosely holding the reins of their mounts and the leads of the mules. Patrick glanced at the others, "Can't see 'em, but I'm sure they're still comin'!" He had untied the captive and roughly slid him to the ground, watched him trying to sit up, his hands tied together.

"We need to find us a good place to make a stand, set up an ambush or sumpin'," whined Smitty, gasping for air. They were nearing timberline and at 12,000 feet, the thin mountain air makes for difficult breathing for flatlanders.

"There's only four of us, and I'm guessin' there's about twenty or more of them," observed Sean, glancing to his cousin for affirmation.

"Yeah, but we've got good rifles," responded Patrick, also sucking air. "And we got him," nodding toward Running Elk. "If he's the chief's son, they won't be too anxious to send a lot of arrows or bullets our way, fear of hittin' him!" He paused, looking at the others, "But these horses…they can't go much further like this and there's still a bit of a climb to get over that saddle behind us."

"The only way we're gonna get over that hump is if we climb ourselves and lead the animals. They can't carry us any further without keelin' over and then we'd really be in a pickle!" answered Smitty. "And I ain't none too anxious to be set afoot in *this* country!"

Patrick stood, looking around them and focused on the mountainside between the long ridge and the taller peak. A natural bowl had formed when some time, eons ago, a big portion of the mountainside sluffed off from the rimrock cliffs that now marked the upper edge of that bowl. The land that had sluffed off, probably after an extended period of rain that turned the mountainside into a big mud pile, now formed a timber-covered shoulder between two scars where runoff water had carved its way to the lower flats and the rivers beyond. Patrick pointed at the rimrock, "There! If we can get above that, the trail there to the left climbs up thataway, then that'll give us natural cover and we can keep anyone from coming up that trail!" He was growing excited as he looked at the trail that sided the end of the ridge and crossed over the saddle between the ridge and the peak. The rimrock and bowl that lay below it, could be a formidable fortress, easily defended.

The others stood, looking where Patrick pointed, and

murmured among themselves until Sean said, "It looks good from here, and with a man on either side of the trail, we can pick 'em off or keep 'em back. Yeah, looks good to me." He turned to look at the long shoulder ridge that stood guard over the flanks of the peak, and to the east at the long ridge they first spotted from the previous night's camp. "And I don't think they can get around behind us. We could even have one or two hang back, keep 'em away, and give the others a chance to get a good distance away, and whoever stayed back wouldn't be draggin' the mules and could prob'ly catch up in short order!" Aiden had followed Sean's gaze, listened to him explain the firing positions and the getaway and was nodding his head in agreement.

Patrick looked at Smitty, "Whaddaya think, Smitty?"

"It ain't like we got a lotta choices, but one things fer shore, if'n we hang around here jawin' too long, we'll lose our hair fer shore! So, I vote we get a move on!" answered the whiskery-faced man as he bent down to pick up the reins of his mount and started up the trail, leading his horse and mule, glancing to their back trail, and struggling with every step. The trail was steep and rocky, forcing the men to use their hands almost as much as their feet as they crawled up the mountainside. The horses and mules picked their way among the slick rocks, zigzagging their way as they followed the men.

THIS WAS THE HOMELAND OF THE MOUACHE UTE PEOPLE, land they had hunted and lived in, mountains they had climbed over and trails they had carved as they followed the elk, deer, and more. They knew this country well and Kaniache held up his hand to stop the others, looking through the break in the trees where the trail led over the saddle between the ridge and the peak. "Red Hawk! Bear Feathers! Come!" he ordered, motioning to the pack of warriors behind him. As the two men came alongside, "Red Hawk, you take four men, go there!" pointing to the long shoulder of the peak, a shoulder that bumped its way west and became a razorback ridge before dropping off into the black timber. The big shoulder was insurmountable with rimrock marking the precipice and dropping off into a long talus slope. But where he pointed, a thin game trail could be seen with its slim line splitting the timber and disappearing around the butte. "Cross over, and come," making a swift motion from the far west back to the peak before them, "The head of that creek a trail crosses there and comes out below the mountain!" indicating the tall peak before them. "Go!" he commanded, watching the man nod and swing his mount around, chose his four warriors and led them onto the trail that cut into the timber.

Kaniache turned, "Bear Feathers—you take four men, go there!" pointing to the aspen-covered mountainside east of the arroyo that scarred the face of the mountain. "Use the trees, go on foot to come behind them on that side." Bear Feathers looked where Kaniache pointed, nodded, and turned back to choose his four warriors. He would have to drop down the hillside where they were, use the trees for cover to make his way into the aspen, then cross the steep hillside. But that would take them high above the trail taken by the white men.

Kaniache stepped down, motioned the others to do the same and the men quickly gathered together in small groups. They shared what little rations they had, mostly pemmican, and sat in the shade to give the other groups time to get into place. They were a patient people and knew they had the advantage over these intruders into their land. They were determined to bring vengeance to bear and looked forward to the opportunity to earn honors among their fellow warriors.

THE SETTING SUN STRETCHED THE SHADOWS OF THE HIGH peak into the valley at its flank. Patrick Matthews was the first to crest the saddle between the mountains. He stood quiet as he took in the vast distances and long line of mountain peaks that stood as pillars of the sky. Each with skirts of black timber covering their flanks as the foothills stretched out to join their strengths and carve the valleys that would carry the runoff from the high mountain crevices that still held glaciers and snowpack. It was a panorama seldom seen by the eyes of white men but one that spoke of the strength and magnificence of the great Creator. He breathed deep of the clear mountain air, thin though it was, it filled his lungs with a freshness never before known. He turned to see the others, standing with the reins of their horses, the leads of the mules held loosely as they, too, took in the expansive view. Distances and views that made the men seem miniscule with everything around them so vast and astounding. Patrick shook his head and looked at the others, "That's sumpin' ain't it?" and chuckled.

He looked down their back trail and saw movement coming from the trees. He guessed them to be about a mile away, but too close for them to dally around and waste time. The natives were coming, and their horses were mountain bred and were accustomed to the high mountains and steep trails. Patrick looked at the others, "We need to decide who's stayin' and who's leavin'!"

Patrick snatched up a twig of kinnikinnick and broke it into four pieces, each of different length. "Two shortest stay, others take him," nodding to the captive, "and the mules and head down country."

"Hold on a minute," pleaded Smitty. "You've got the map an' you said this hyar mountain was the one with the treasure, somewhere. So, who keeps the map, them what stays or them what goes?"

Patrick looked at Running Elk, "Where's that waterfall?"

Elk let a slow grin split his face, nodded to the peak above them and the trail they just climbed, "Back there," pointing beyond the mountain. "Two days."

"But don't the map say this is the mountain?" asked Smitty, looking to Patrick.

"Yes, but the trail or clues to the treasure, start at the waterfall. So, it must be on the other side of this mountain."

"I don't see that it makes any difference. Those that stay behind, won't stay long, just long enough to discourage those comin' after us. Then hurry up and catch up to the rest," explained Sean. He glanced to his cousin, nodded, and turned back to Smitty and Patrick, "Me'n Aiden will stay behind, leave the spare rifles from Leck and Lemmon, and we'll do our best to convince the Indians to leave us alone or at least to keep their distance. Then we'll follow after you." He glanced to the sky, saw the sun was just about to tuck itself away for the night, and added, "Dark'll be here soon and there's a full moon tonight, so we'll catch up after dark. Just keep watchin' for us and don't shoot us for Indians!"

Smitty looked at Patrick who nodded his agreement, and Smitty quickly pulled the spare rifles from the packs, grabbed the leads of the mules led by the cousins, and started down the trail, Patrick following. Sean looked at his cousin, "Which side do you want?" looking at the rimrock and other cover.

"I'll take the rocks and trees yonder. You can stay here in the open and keep 'em away from the trees!"

"From what we've seen so far, they might take a bit of convincin'. If you see 'em first, wait till you have an open shot, then lay it on 'em. I'll do the same!" He watched as Aiden turned away, a rifle in each hand, and started to the trees beyond the trail. He looked around, chose a big flat-topped boulder, and took his position. The horses were tethered in the oak brush behind them, well out of sight and behind cover. Now, it was just waiting.

26 / *SKIRMISH*

The cousins had placed their spare rifles about ten feet away, choosing to give the appearance of more shooters with fire coming from two positions. Now they both sat, Sean behind the big boulder and looking down the shoulder below the trail, Aiden behind a sizable aspen as he overlooked the east rise of the trail. They were of similar minds, patient and waiting for the right shot to have the greatest effect and impact on the attackers. But waiting is never easy, especially when your life and your future appear to be less certain than the low clouds that hung near the tip of the peak.

Aiden was the first to detect movement, but not from the trail. Faint shadows, barely visible in the light of dusk, flitted through the white pillars along the face of the hillside. They were too far away to be certain, and the trees too thick for a good shot, but he felt, more than saw, them coming toward him. He scanned the trail below and turned to face the apparitions that moved through the trees. With the white bark of the aspen and the quaking pale-green leaves, the attackers had less cover than they would in a pine forest. Aiden focused on an opening through the trees that pierced the grove and gave him a view deeper into the shaded hillside. He had Mickey Lemmon's Spencer and eared back the hammer, let his breath come easy and when the shadow moved between the white trunks, he dropped the hammer.

The smoke belched and the Spencer roared, shattering the stillness. The thud of a strike was accented by the scream of the warrior. As the echo of the blast bounced across the vale, Aiden had already jacked another cartridge into the chamber and brought the hammer to full cock. He searched for another target, saw movement, and fired again. He thought he saw the figure stumble and fall, but the smoke from the muzzle and the dim light of dusk made him uncertain. With another cartridge in the chamber, he leaned the Spencer against the tree, and scampered to the other rifle, lower down the hill but behind a ponderosa.

Sean heard the shot of his cousin and saw the shoulder of an attacker behind a boulder below him. He paused a moment until the warrior began to move around the big rock and he fired. The Henry blasted, the crack of the shot made a clattering echo, but the bullet flew true, and Sean saw the warrior grab at his chest and stumble to fall on his face. Before the man hit the ground, Sean had jacked another cartridge into the chamber and was picking his next target, a warrior who pushed through some scrub oak, and was met with the driving force of lead from the Henry that splattered his face with blood, jerked his head back and drove him to the ground.

The two cousins continued their barrage of rifle fire, Sean with his two Henrys, Aiden with the Spencer and a Henry, and gave the impression there were at least four riflemen and maybe more. Gun smoke lifted in a wispy cloud above the boulders that protected Sean, and filtered through the aspen where Aiden, now on one knee behind the ponderosa, had taken cover. With the rattle of gunfire, and the constant reverberation of the echoes, sometimes several for each shot, the saddle between the ridge and peak sounded like a battleground where two armies had clashed.

Screamed war cries from the Mouache, rifle fire from the few with muskets, and the clatter of arrows bouncing off boulders added to the mayhem, yet the constant barrage of rifle fire had stayed the attack by the Mouache. The warriors had dropped behind the cover of boulders and trees, unwilling to needlessly sacrifice themselves and the thunderous roar of battle began to subside. The rifle fire from above the attackers had dwindled to scattered shots, yet the echoes still magnified the blasts of gunfire.

The cousins had agreed to signal one another with the two-toned whistle of the yellow-bellied marmot, and the signal was sounded by Sean. Aiden heard, worked back uphill beside the trail, and dropped to a crouch to cross over to the horses. Sean was loosing the tethers as Aiden came near and was about to mount when an arrow whispered between them. Both men dropped to a crouch, looked to the west along the shoulder of the big peak and saw two warriors starting to charge at them.

Sean, still holding a Henry in one hand, lifted it and fired pistol-style, dropping the nearest warrior. Aiden was slipping the Spencer into the scabbard and grabbed the Henry that lay across the saddle and brought it to bear on the second man. He fired, saw the man stumble, and swung into the saddle just as Sean stuck a foot in the stirrup and both horses lunged away from the brush.

Sean struggled to gain his seat and let his horse have his head as it took to the trail at an all-out run.

The men dropped low on the necks of their mounts, manes whipping their faces, and the horses took the trail like it was the home stretch to a long journey. The narrow trail began to twist through the timber and the men had to dip and duck to keep from getting knocked off their saddles by low-hanging limbs and close-encountered trees. The horses slowed the pace but little, until they broke into a bit of a clearing where a small stream parted the willows and trickled over the rocks. The men pulled the horses to a walk, sat up in their saddles and twisted around to look at their back trail.

The Ute had all approached their attack on foot, choosing stealth over speed, but now their quarry had escaped. At the shouted commands of Red Hawk and Bear Feathers, the warriors ran back to retrieve their mounts. Kaniache had left two younger warriors with their horses and the command was relayed back and now they came at a run, dragging the horses behind them. Within moments, Kaniache had rallied the three bands at the crest of the saddle and as he looked at the warriors, he noticed several missing. "Yellow Nose, you and Wounded Bear take two others, gather the dead and injured and return to the village."

The two warriors nodded, turned their mounts back from the others, gathered the horses of the downed, and began searching for the dead. Two were walking wounded, and at Wounded Bear's motion, they mounted and started back together. One man showed blood at his side, the other had blooded leggings. They watched as the rest of the war party took to the trail and disappeared into the trees.

THE RATTLE OF RIFLE FIRE ROLLED LIKE THUNDER FROM the high country. Reuben looked to Elly, shook his head, "Sounds like a war!" In the high country, the blast of gunfire carries a long distance in the thin air, added to the echoes, the rumble of thunder rolled down the mountains and filtered through the valleys to be caught and muffled by the tall standing timber.

"That must be from the white men, I didn't see many rifles among the Mouache," replied Elly. She was sitting up, holding a steaming cup of coffee in her hands, and savoring the smell. They had enjoyed their feast of turkey and the sumptuous meal had helped Elly regain her strength and grit. She looked at Reuben, "By morning, I think I'll be able to ride. Don't you think we should go after them," nodding to the mountain behind them, "just in case they're still alive and the Ute might turn 'em over to us?"

"Well, I don't think there's much chance of that, but even if they are still alive and captives, Kaniache probably won't turn 'em over."

"Shouldn't we try? After all, they're no different than any other gold hunter."

"How many other gold hunters do you know that took a chief's son captive?"

"Oh, yeah."

"And how many other gold hunters do you know that tried to kill my wife?"

"But they didn't!"

"That doesn't change the fact that they tried, or at least one of 'em did!" He dropped to one knee beside her and looked at her, "I know all about forgiveness and not passing judgment on someone, but 'tween you and me and that rock over there, it scared the buhjeebies outta me to see you layin' in the dirt, bleedin' and unconscious. I thought you were dead! And I don't ever want to feel that again."

Elly looked into the eyes of her man, a slow smile painting her face and said, "I love you too, and I know how you felt because I've felt that same way when you were shot. But that doesn't change things. We're still deputy marshals and we have a job to do, even if we don't like it! And right now, that job says we need to see about gettin' those men back from the Mouache."

Reuben was quiet a moment, lifted his eyes to hers and said, "We're not goin' anywhere tonight. If you're doin' better in the mornin' then we'll see if we can get the gold hunters back. For right now, you're gonna get some rest, but first, I've got to check your wound and bandages. I'm sure they'll need changin' and that means you need to lie down and let me play nursemaid!"

27 / CHANGES

It was a restless night. Although the star-filled sky was clear and cool, Elly did not rest well. When Reuben felt her brow, she was feverish and by early morning, she had become delirious, kicking off the blanket, mumbling and crying in her sleep, such as it was. Reuben tried to check the wound by the firelight, but just his touch caused her to cry out in pain. When first light showed, he held her thrashing arms, fought to remove the bandage, and when he pulled it away, he saw her entire side was inflamed and swollen.

"I'm gonna hafta cut those stitches and drain the wound. It's infected and inflamed and it needs cleanin'," he declared, speaking as much to himself as to the incoherent and feverish Elly. "And I need some whiskey or somethin' to wash out that wound and I ain't got nuthin'!" He was mumbling as he looked around, searching for anything that would help. He stood, walked to the fire, and picked up the coffee pot, dumped it out and went to the creek for fresh water. He set the pot in the coals and went to the medicine kit. Although Elly had often mixed a special concoction with the Balm of Gilead taken from the shoots of the aspen to make her ointment, she also had some of those shoots separate and he picked several, dropping them into the coffee pot. He added some bear root and some sage and some willow twigs to the mix and let the water come to a boil.

After it brewed for a little bit, he returned to Elly's side, coffee pot in hand and a clean swatch of linen. Setting them to the side, he lifted her tunic to reveal the bandaged wound and gently removed the bandage to begin rinsing the now-opened wound with the special tea. He used the fresh cloth to wipe the wound clear of any puss or detritus, rinsing it again and sat back. "I think I'll leave that open to the air for a bit, clean it again after it dries, then bandage it again without stitching it closed. Maybe it'll drain while its open." He spoke aloud just in case the seemingly unconscious Elly could hear and maybe understand, the words also voicing his thoughts and giving him a little solace.

After the second cleansing, he left the wound open to the air and sat back to watch. She had not moved nor spoken since he started working the wound, but she was no longer delirious nor restless. Although he had spent most of the night in prayer, he sat back on the big rock above her and renewed his prayer with a heartfelt fervency, pleading with God for his mercy and healing. He had no sooner said 'Amen' than he saw Elly stirring. He dropped to his knees beside her, looking at her face and glancing to the wound. Her eyes fluttered and she started to smile, winced, and started to feel her wound, but Reuben stopped her. "Don't! I've got to change your bandage and you can't touch it." His hand protected the wound as he looked at her.

"It hurts," she said, frowning and looking about.

"Yeah, it got infected a mite, but I've cleaned it out

and we'll leave it open for a bit longer. I'm gonna saddle the horses and pack up. Dependin' on what you can handle, I'll either have you in my saddle, me behind to hold you, and we'll ride outta here, or I'll fashion a travois and haul you out. Either way, we're goin' to the fort, let the company surgeon take a look at that," nodding to her side.

"Let's do the saddle. Travois is a last resort, and I don't cotton to the idea of bouncin' along behind!"

"DID YOU HEAR ALL THAT SHOOTIN' BACK THERE?" ASKED Smitty as he moved up beside Patrick and the captive.

"Course I did! I ain't deef!" declared Patrick. They had stopped in a bit of a clearing where the creek passed through, splitting the willows and oak brush. "We haven't come that far, but we need to keep movin' cuz if they didn't get 'em stopped, they'll be comin' up on us real soon!" He twisted around in his saddle, one hand on the cantle as he looked to their back trail. He turned back around, looked at Running Elk, "If we follow that crick in the bottom, can we come back around to the waterfall?"

Elk frowned, looking at the strange white man, and slowly nodded. "Yes. That stream cuts through these mountains and joins the one that flows from the valley where the waterfall drops its water."

"How far?"

"Less than a day." He looked to the dim light of dusk, "Maybe when the moon is high."

Patrick looked at Smitty and smiled, "Ya hear that? We could get to the waterfall 'fore midnight!"

"Yeah, but can we see any o' the clues, you know, like the fleur-de-lis?"

"If we find the waterfall, we can hide out till mornin' then go the rest o' the way. Now, let's get a move on, Sean and Aiden'll be comin' along soon 'nuff."

Patrick had tied the mules together in a long string, leads to tails, and let Smitty do the leading of all the mules while he handled the captive. He nudged his mount forward and they resumed their trek, hopeful of leaving the Indians behind and finding their treasure. Hope and greed were crowding out fear and common sense.

THE GLOW OF THE SETTING SUN PAINTED THE WESTERN SKY in muted colors of gold and orange that were quickly fading as the dim light of dusk crowded out the colors. With the curtain of darkness slowly lowering, shadows dimmed and the glow of a rising full moon cast the pale light along the valley floor. Patrick and the captive, followed closely by Smitty trailing the pack mules, rode from the trees into the open grassy flats of the valley bottom, relieved to see the openness and the trail that clearly sided the river. This was the East Fork of the San Juan River that meandered through the valley, with sandy shoals at most every bend, and at no place was the river much wider than fifty feet and at its deepest it was maybe three feet, except in the back-water pools on the undercut bends.

The trail kept to the north side of the west-bound river, cutting through the willows and spindly hackberry trees. Across the river, another shoulder of the mountain had sluffed off and slid toward the river bottom but was now covered mostly with aspen. The end of one shoulder showed a steep cliff that stood above the talus slope and ended abruptly as it dropped into the black timber. Patrick looked to Running Elk, "How much further to the valley where your village lies?"

Running Elk leaned to the side as if trying to see around the far bend that shielded the rest of the river bottom, and said, "Not far, soon."

"Good. I wanna find that waterfall 'fore daylight. Then we can make camp."

"Will you let me go then?" asked the captive.

"Maybe later. Don't want you to go runnin' to your people, tellin' 'em where we are."

Running Elk let his lip curl in a snarl as he glared at his captor. He wanted to jump from his mount and run into the trees, but he knew he could not make it far with his splinted and broken leg. He was at their mercy, and they kept his hands tied and bound to the mane of his horse.

Behind them, the sound of running horses crashing through the brush warned them of pursuit. Patrick motioned to the tree line and drove his mount into the shadows. Smitty struggled with the lagging mules but was soon hidden in the trees just moments before their pursuers were seen. It was the cousins, and Patrick called to them, "Here! In the trees!"

The two riders came to a stop, looked to the trees, and nudged their mounts closer. Patrick asked, "Are they followin'?"

"Prob'ly. We dropped a couple, wounded a couple. They had split up and come at us from below and both sides. We almost didn't get outta there. Haven't heard anything behind us yet, but we were makin' so much noise there could be a herd of stampedin' elephants and we wouldn't know it!" answered Sean.

"Then we need to keep goin'. The Injun says we can make the waterfall by midnight an' we can make camp near there, if it ain't too close to the village. But I ain't lettin' nuthin' keep us from that treasure, even if we have ta' kill all of 'em in that village!" growled Patrick, his frustration digging in deep.

The trail hugged the creek until the mountains pushed in and narrowed the valley into a steep-walled canyon. The game trail they followed had been carved over the years, perhaps millennia, and hung like an eyebrow on the steep hillside that at times was nothing more than a cliff face. The clatter of hooves echoed across the canyon, muffled only by the chuckling of the river over the shallows and cascades as it tumbled from the high country, working its way to meet up with the waters from Wolf Creek and the West Fork of the San Juan. The mountains slid back as the trail rounded a point and broke into the wider valley where the confluence of rivers could be seen as the moonlight bounced off the marriage of the waters. The trail pointed back into the bigger valley, but they were stopped by the sudden appearance of a dozen warriors, sitting their horses, and glaring at the white intruders. Patrick started to grab his rifle but was stopped by Smitty, "Don't! They'll kill us sure!"

His words had scarcely dropped before the Indians surrounded them with some grabbing at their gear while others kept them still with the tips of lances pressed against their chests or bow with nocked arrows pointed at them. At the motion of the leader, the men raised their hands high and were quickly jerked from their horses. Several of the warriors grabbed at the reins of the mounts and the leads of the mules and led them from the trail, disappearing into the trees. Warriors grabbed the wrists of the men, jerked them behind them and bound them. Once they were secure, the leader shouted orders to the others and the men were prodded forward to follow the other mounted warriors into the trees.

The frightened men kept looking at one another, their captors, and the trees, searching for any way to escape, but they were bound tight and held by at least one captor. "What're they gonna do?" whined Smitty, looking at the others.

"How should I know?" answered Patrick, stumbling, and jerked back to his feet by two warriors that held his arms.

Sean was watching the men and noticed Running Elk had been freed but was walking beside another warrior, using his shoulder for support as he limped on the leg that had the splint. As Sean looked around, it seemed there were suddenly more warriors than those that had stopped them on the trail. He saw one man, impressive as he walked before the others, with his hair pipe bone breastplate, etched silver bands on his biceps, and hair pipe bone choker. His hair held several feathers standing tall in the scalp lock. Long braids fell over his shoulders and accented his deep chest and broad shoulders. His stoic expression showed eyes full of hatred as he growled to the captives, "Who took my son?"

Running Elk came to the side of his father, spoke softly to the man, and nodded toward Patrick. Kaniache looked at his son, "Who did that?"

"I fell under a horse, the horse broke my leg, but the big one at the rear," nodding to Sean, "fixed the splint to heal my leg."

Again, the chief glowered at Patrick, looked at Sean, and turned back to his son. He spoke to his son with his back to the captives, and within moments, the chief barked orders to the warriors. Patrick and Smitty were pushed back against a pair of ponderosa, their arms bent behind them, and wrists bound together. Another warrior wrapped rawhide around one ankle, took the rawhide behind the tree and tied off the other ankle. Both men were tight against the rough bark of the tall ponderosa and if their weight sagged, it pulled against the rawhide, making it even tighter. A warrior brought a gourd of water and soaked the rawhide bindings, giving a moment's relief to the captors, but both men realized when the rawhide began to dry, the shrinking bonds would draw tighter and tighter.

Kaniache and Running Elk stood before Sean and Aiden, both men with hands tied behind them, a warrior on each side holding their arms. Kaniache spoke in English, "You showed kindness to my son when you tended his leg. You both have shown your bravery in battle. You will be released, but before you go, you must run the line of women." He looked at the warriors, barked orders to them, and the men began stripping off the shoes and shirts of the two captives, cutting the shirts in strips to remove them without removing the bonds. Kaniache added, "The women of the village will tend to those," nodding to Patrick and Smitty, "and they will join the men for the line of women. When the sun rises, this will be done." He glared at the men, turned, and walked away. His son, with the aid of the other man, followed his father.

28 / FLIGHT

The night seemed endless, the men were within sight of each other, but words were hard to come by as hopelessness began to crawl into their minds. By the first light of day, they had slumped in their bonds, trying to escape into slumber, but a short and uncomfortable snooze was all that came. Three warriors came into the little clearing before them, each one carrying an armload of firewood and they dropped it all into a pile. Another man brought a firebrand from their cookfire and stuffed it into the pile, scattering dry pine needles on top and within moments, the needles smoldered and caught, tiny flames licking up at the wood. As the flames began to hungrily devour the pile, long tongues of fire chased away the shadows of early morning, the heat welcomed by the bound men who had shivered through most of the night.

But the arrival of women that came in bunches, chattering among themselves, excited for the coming events, brought the attention of the men from the fire to the women, some with tear-filled eyes still grieving the loss of their men, all with anger flaming from their eyes. One woman, attired more like a warrior than a woman, stood before them, arms outstretched and began to talk to the crowd, anger flaring as she spoke, often motioning to the captives. As she finished, she stepped aside and the crowd of women, probably as many as fifty or sixty, surged forward, several grabbing firebrands from the raging fire, others already bearing willow withes, war clubs, and more.

All the women were attired much the same, beaded and fringed buckskin tunics, some also with leggings, all with beaded moccasins. Many had blankets wrapped around their shoulders like a shawl, some with hair hanging loosely, some with braids decorated with tufts of dyed rabbit fur, a few with headbands, all carrying some sort of weapon in their hands. As they approached the men, most went to Patrick and Smitty and began shouting and screaming as they lashed out with the willow withes, whipping at the men's faces. Those with firebrands held the fiery end against the chests and necks of the men, some drove them into their crotches, laughing and cackling as they struck. Most would scream and spit on the men, some reached out to slap them or hit them with fists. The few with war clubs were merciless and struck the men about their head and shoulders repeatedly until their faces and upper torsos were covered with blood. The two men's eyes had swollen almost shut and they could not see for the blood and more.

None of those with firebrands came against the cousins, but several with willow whips attacked them. Since they had been freed of their shirts and stood bare chested, their chests, necks, and faces were soon covered with red welts and thin courses of blood. It was futile to try to duck away from the blows and both men stood tall and strong, eyes closed, as they took the whippings. The torture seemed to last for hours but in truth it was no more than fifteen minutes before the women stepped away, mocking and jeering at the weak white men that were bleeding. Patrick and Smitty were sobbing and drooping in pain.

Sean looked to Aiden, "Did you notice how only the women with willow whips came after us? Those older women with the torches went after those two, but not us!"

Aiden struggled to speak, having been struck in the throat numerous times, but he choked out the words, "I did...they're savin' us for somethin', prob'ly worse!"

"What do you s'pose is that 'line of women' the chief mentioned?"

"Dunno, but if it's worse'n this, I ain't none too anxious to find out."

As they watched, two warriors came with water bags and poured water over Patrick and Smitty, giving little relief but bringing them back to full consciousness. Both men tried to stand but had been so weakened by the torture, they slumped again against their bonds, knees bent, heads drooping, barely breathing.

Sean and Aiden watched the men, fearing their time was coming and they too would experience the brunt of the attacks by the women, but Kaniache strode into the clearing with his son, Running Elk, still using another for support behind him. The chief and his son glanced at Patrick and Smitty and walked to face Sean and Aiden. They stood before them, feet well apart, shoulders back, and eyes squinting as they glared at the two cousins—the son the image of his father.

Kaniache nodded and said, "You have done well, but now it is your time." He motioned toward the men, four warriors came from behind him and began untying their bonds. With one man on each arm, the cousins were led away from the trees and into the open meadow of the lower end of the large park where the village stood in the upper end. Two lines of women, standing close beside one another, bearing the same weapons used on the others, stood before them, taunting and jeering as the two cousins were led closer.

Kaniache stood beside them and pointed to the upper end of the valley, a distance of about three miles, "There is the trail from this valley." Where he pointed was the northwest edge of the valley above the village. "If you survive this," nodding to the two lines of the women, "you will leave this land. There, at the end of the line, is one knife in the ground, take it and go. Warriors will follow to be certain you leave; they may try to kill you. It is up to you to leave and live."

The cousins looked at one another, both bare chested and barefooted, with fear showing in their eyes. Sean said, "We can do this, just keep your head down and move as fast as you can. I'll go first, but don't be too far behind me."

Sean walked a little closer, looked down the line that he guessed to be about twenty-five yards, maybe a little longer, and with women spaced out about a yard between them. All were brandishing some kind of club or willow whip; all were shouting and jeering. He looked back at Kaniache who nodded and motioned for him to go. He looked down the line again, glanced to his cousin and bent low, and leaped to start his run.

The first women were surprised at his start and did not get in good licks, but the others did their best to compensate, screaming and swinging. He lifted his arms high to protect his head and face, but plunged on, feeling the crushing blows, and wincing with the pain. He stumbled and fell, but caught himself as several women swarmed around him trying to beat him into the ground. He swung blindly, felt his fist strike one then another, and plunged on. One woman stepped in front of him with a massive war club raised high, but he bowled her over, stepped over her, and kept going. One club came down on the back of his neck as he was bent low, and he put out his hands to keep from going down, used them to keep his footing and lunged forward away from the club. Several women, bunched together, had rawhide whips, and repeatedly struck him, cutting the flesh on his back, and blood coursed across his form making him look like a bloody ogre. He stood, lifted his hands, and screamed, spinning around and striking at anything close. He lunged again, seeing the end of the line in reach and drove himself forward, leaping past the last woman and continuing until he felt no more strikes. He slowed, turned to see Aiden fighting the same line and began cheering him on, "You can do it! Come on Aiden, come on!" he screamed, bent over with hands on his knees and breathing hard. It hurt to watch Aiden take blow after blow and stumble and fall, for he had often protected his cousin like a brother. When Aiden was down, the women swarmed around, clubs uplifted and striking. Sean screamed and charged into the melee, taking more blows but determined to reach his cousin. He dropped to one knee, grabbed Aiden by the armpits, lifted him and spun around, pulling him up on his back, all the while suffering blow upon blow. He staggered to the end of the line, Aiden's body taking most of the blows, but they cleared the end of the line and kept going until silence came. Sean turned, Aiden's arms over his shoulders and chin on his shoulder, and looked back at the women who stood, watching and quiet.

Sean turned and started walking toward the distant goal. He could feel Aiden's breath on his shoulder, and he spoke, "Hang on Aiden, we can make it, just hang on." He staggered and stumbled, breathing deep, feeling the pain of his wounds. His left eye had swollen almost shut and he had to cock his head and lift his chin to be able to see the trail. Trees draped the hillside to his right, tall grass waved across the valley floor and riders came from the village, ignoring the white man carrying the bloody form on his back, bound for the lower camp where the torture of captives was continuing.

Sean thought of Patrick and Smitty, shook his head at the image of the bloodied men, but knew he and Aiden would be lucky if they made it out of this land alive. Every step reminded him he was barefoot, but he thought it could be a lot worse. As a lad, he had seldom worn shoes, but the last few years with hobnail boots had softened the soles of his feet, but he chose his steps, keeping to the grass, hoping his feet would soon harden and he could walk without pain.

Aiden stirred, "Sean? Sean? Put me down."

Sean turned to look back toward the lower encampment, saw no one following and walked closer to the tree line and stopped under a big ponderosa to slowly let Aiden down to the ground, letting him drop to the deep cushion of long pine needles. Aiden struggled to sit, watched Sean sit beside him, and the men looked at one another, turned to look back down the trail and Aiden said, "Thanks. I thought I was done in, and they were gonna kill me."

"They almost did! I thought they'd kill both of us."

"Makes me want to never look at another woman for

as long as I live!" growled Aiden, his voice raspy from the blows to his throat.

"Before we started, I was thankful it was women instead of the men, but I dunno…" he shrugged, chuckling. He looked at his cousin, shook his head, "We need to do somethin' about our wounds, but first, we need to get outta this valley. Looks to be about two miles to that trail between the buttes, think you can make it?"

"I reckon it's do or die, ain't it?"

"Ummhmmm."

They got to their feet, Sean helping Aiden to stand, and with Aiden's hand on his shoulder, Sean started walking. It was slow going, but after another mile, they started to stop when Sean frowned, listening, and stepped away from the trees to look up the hillside. He grinned slowly, motioned to Aiden to come alongside and when they stood shoulder to shoulder, he pointed to the mountain. There, about two hundred yards up the hillside where a long shoulder of rim rock and cliffs cut across the face of the hill, a stream dropped from the upper reaches and cascaded down a long waterfall, splitting the face of the cliff and crashing onto the rocks below. The stream came from the face of the hillside, cascading down the steep slope to cross the trail no more than a few feet from where they stood.

Aiden looked at Sean and back to the waterfall, and said, "You don't s'pose…?" and looked back at his cousin who stood grinning and nodding his head. "Yup, I'm thinkin' that's the waterfall we were chasin', the one on the treasure map."

29 / TREK

They knew they were in for a long ride, the fort was at least two days, more likely three days travel, but they could stay on the trail and make good time with their trail-proven horses. Reuben had lifted Elly into the saddle and now sat behind her, the cantle between them, and with both arms around her, he loosely held the reins in his left hand and nudged Blue to the trail. Bear had taken point and was leading the way, looking over his shoulder a little more often to ensure they were still following. He was obviously concerned about Elly, for the two of them had always been close and he often slept beside her.

Daisy, Elly's appaloosa mare, was on a lead directly behind Blue, but the mule, as was often done, came free rein and did his best to stay beside Blue on the trail, for they had been trail buddies since they first traveled together and had covered many miles and a lot of country in that time. The sun had climbed high in the sky when they broke from the canyon and into the flats where the South Fork merged with the Rio Bravo, or Rio Grande. It was a good time to take their nooning and

Reuben chose a point just below the confluence, a grassy flat where few willows sided the big river, and the open valley was a pleasant change.

After lifting Elly to the ground and making a bit of a palette for her, Reuben gathered wood for a fire and put the freshly filled coffee pot on the rock beside the small fire. He dug in their parfleche for some fresh meat and hung it over the fire on some sticks of willow. "That's the last of the meat. I'm either gonna hafta get some fresh meat, or maybe go fishin'," he drawled as he dropped a handful of fresh ground coffee into the pot.

"Since we'll be near the water most of the day, how 'bout we just keep our eyes open for somethin' by the river?" suggested Elly, wincing with pain and trying to get comfortable on the pad of blankets.

"You're hurtin' aren't you?"

"Yeah, but I'll be alright."

"After that coffee perks and we have some, I'll brew up some o' that tea and stuff, clean your wound and change your bandages." He walked over to the willows, cut a couple of small twigs, and peeled back the bark. A glance to the side showed a plant with white blossoms that Reuben recognized as meadowsweet, and he plucked several of the blooms. Returning to Elly, he handed the willow twigs to her, "Chew on that a while."

She frowned when she saw the blooms held in the other hand and looked up at Reuben, "Is that meadowsweet?"

"It is. Gonna add these to the brew I'll make in a bit, might help with your pain."

"It will. I'm glad you found it."

After they had eaten, Reuben turned to Elly, "You need to stretch out and lay back so I can work on your wound."

She smiled, sighed heavily as she stretched out and steeled herself for what was coming. She had felt the wound as she rode, feeling the stabbing pains with each rough step, and had felt the bandage become wet, knowing she was bleeding, but was not concerned, knowing the draining of the wound was necessary. When Reuben pulled the bandage away, she could see in his eyes he was not pleased. "It stinks, and it's not lookin' real good. We're gonna hafta wash it out better, don't know about sewin' it up though." The skin around the wound was still inflamed, some showing the purple of bruising, but the slight discoloration closer to the wound concerned him most. He touched the flesh, she winced and frowned, "That's good. You can still feel it." He had brewed some more medicinal tea with the Balm of Gilead, sage, willow bark, and the added meadowsweet. As he grabbed a clean linen swatch, he poured the warm mixture on the wound, carefully cleaning it all, and rinsed it again. Elly was struggling with the pain but withstood the treatment, though not with a smile. Once the wound was clean, he worked at replacing the bandage, using Elly's medicinal ointment, and binding her as tight as possible so the bandage would stay in place while they rode.

He tossed the remainder of the cleansing brew and with a pot of fresh water, brewed her some meadowsweet tea, using some of the leaves and the blossoms for their pain-relieving qualities. By the time he was finished, and she had downed most of the tea, Reuben was tightening the cinches on the saddles and packs and readying the animals. He looked at Elly, "You wanna stay in the saddle or you want me to make a travois?"

"Saddle, you can hold me close and that'll make me feel better," she smiled and winked at him, knowing he was worried about her and doing his best to take care of her and get her to the fort and the doctor.

The sun was dropping behind the mountains behind them when they rode clear of the mountains and into the flats of the San Luis Valley. Some low foothills, mesas, and buttes shouldered in from the south side of the river, but they had crossed over to the north bank where a gravel-bottomed shallow offered an easy crossing. They knew they would be traveling on the north bank of the river across the flats, and nearer the fort the river would bend south as they continued east. Reuben was looking for a campsite among the cottonwoods when Elly, who had been snoozing as she leaned against her man, roused, and asked, "Are we stopping already?"

"Yeah, I thought you'd like to stretch out and get some rest."

"How much farther to the fort?"

"A good day's travel, maybe a little more."

"Then let's do the 'little more' now while we can, 'fore dark," suggested Elly.

"You sure you can take it?"

"Yeah, long as you hold me tight!" she twisted around to smile at her man and lifted her hand to his cheek.

"I can do that!" he declared, smiling, and hugging her close.

Dusk was surrendering to the darkness when Elly pointed at a cluster of cottonwoods and said, "I'm gettin' hungry and tired. So, how 'bout we stop there?"

"Suits me!" declared Reuben, using leg pressure to nudge Blue into the grove. It didn't take long to get camp set up and a fire going, but their supper amounted to a stew of pemmican, onions, timpsila, and cattail shoots. But when hunger calls, just about anything can answer, and the two weary travelers were soon satisfied. As

Reuben sipped coffee, Elly sipped meadowsweet tea and they both were soon ready for the blankets.

The rattle of trace chains and creak of wagon wheels caught their attention and Reuben stood, grabbed up his Henry and motioned for Elly to stay on the blankets. He walked to the edge of the trees to see two wagons and several riders pulling into the nearby clearing at the edge of the trees. Reuben stepped behind a tree and watched as they began setting up their camp and hailed the camp as he moved closer, "Hello the camp! I'm friendly and comin' in!"

"Come ahead on but keep your hands where we can see 'em!" came a voice from beyond the wagons. He walked closer, noted two women busy at building a fire, four men, two younger, busy with the animals. One man stood by the first wagon—rifle loosely held across his chest as he watched the visitor approach.

Reuben nodded, held his rifle at his side, "I'm Reuben Grundy. My wife and I are camped just through there." Nodding in the direction of their camp, unseen through the thicket. "Thought I'd check in on you 'fore somebody started shootin' our direction, thinkin' we were deer or sumpin'."

"Ah, we wouldn't do that! Anybody that can't see what they're shootin' at and still pulls the trigger should be shot his own self!" declared the man by the wagon. "Grundy is it?"

"That's right."

"Well, we're the Donavan's, all of us. I'm John, that big fella yonder is my brother, Matthew," the big man waved one hand but continued working on the harness of the mules, "The two younger ones are Luke and John, and that'n over yonder is our friend, Rastus!" Reuben looked to the other man, surprised to see he was colored, but the man smiled broadly, nodded, and continued with the animals.

"Well, we prob'ly won't see much of you, my wife's not feeling well and we're on our way to the fort to see the doctor there, so we'll be leavin' early." He paused, looking around and noticed the similarity of the clothing, the men all had flat brimmed, round-crowned black hats, black trousers with black galluses, and blue shirts. Both of the women had small bonnets and pale-blue dresses. Neither paid much attention to their visitor.

Reuben asked, "You folks travelin' far?"

"Not far. Lookin' for some farmland. Are you familiar with this country?"

"Yes, a little. Best country for farming that I've seen so far is right across the river. Good land, fertile soil, and water close by. You should know this country is not like back east, you can't raise many crops on rainwater. This land doesn't get much. But if you can manage some irrigation water, you might do alright."

"Well, thank you friend. That's good to hear," answered John, nodding and stepping forward as if pushing Reuben away.

Reuben grinned, nodded, and said, "Well, you folks have a fine evening," tipped his hat to the ladies and turned to leave. He shook his head slightly, grinning at the mistrust some people show, and returned to his camp.

Come morning, Elly was restless and feverish. Reuben checked and changed the bandages, cleaning the wound, and gave her some more of the tea. They were on the trail early and the flat lands promised an easier day of travel. The sun was warm and the travel easy, with a short stop for nooning and resting the animals, but they were soon on the trail again. By dusk, they were riding into the compound of Fort Garland and Captain Kerber stepped from his office to greet them just as Reuben stepped to the ground and lifted Elly from the saddle.

"Howdy captain, is the doc around?" asked Reuben, letting Elly lean against Blue as he tethered the animals.

The captain turned to his aid and ordered him to fetch the company surgeon, turned back to Reuben, frowning, "What happened?"

"Kind of a long story, I'd like to get Elly settled first. Can we use the same quarters?"

"Certainly, certainly. May I be of help?"

"If you could get someone to see to the horses and mule, maybe bring our gear to the quarters, that'd be a help. I need to help her," nodding to Elly who was leaning on Reuben's shoulder.

"I'll see to that. Will you give me a report soon?"

"You can come to the quarters if you want, once the doc takes over, I'll be glad to fill you in."

"Good, good," responded the captain, watching Reuben practically carry Elly down the line of officer's quarters to the one on the end where they stayed before. He kicked open the door and helped her inside. He had no sooner laid her on the bed than the doctor rapped on the door and entered, bag in hand.

"What's the problem?"

"She was shot a couple days ago, a deep graze on her side there. Been tendin' it, but it don't seem to be gettin' any better."

"I'll take a look. Could you get me some fresh water heating up, please?"

"Will do!" answered Reuben, turning away, yet smiling at Elly to reassure her.

A short while later, the doctor told Reuben, "It's good

you got her to me. It was showing a little infection, but I took care of that, took a couple stitches, and I think she'll be fine. I'll check back in the morning after she's had some rest."

"Thanks doc," answered Reuben, shaking his hand as he started for the door.

Once the doctor had left, he stepped into the bedroom and sat on the side of the bed. Elly was smiling and reached out her hand, "I'll be fine. Doc said so!"

"You better. Now you get some sleep. I'll check on the horses and talk to the captain, but I'll be back soon." Elly nodded, turned to her side, and smiled as Reuben left the room.

30 / RESOLVE

Elly awoke to the smell of coffee brewing and bacon sizzling. She smiled, rolled over, and stretched, wincing at the pain in her side, but relieved it was not as bad as before, and kicked off the covers to throw her legs over the side of the bed and stood. It felt good to be on her feet, and she pushed open the door and peeked out to see Reuben standing over the stove, tending the cooking. She tiptoed up behind him, wrapped her arms around him and hugged him close to her.

"Whooaa, who's that tryin' to hogtie me?" drawled Reuben as he turned around to face his wife. He chuckled as she lay her head on his chest. "Does this mean you're feelin' better?"

"It does! And you're feelin' good to me as well!" she giggled, her arms around his waist as she leaned against him, looking up at him and smiling.

"Well, you better let the cook go, or you won't have anything for breakfast!"

"What're we havin' besides coffee and bacon?"

"What else do you need?" he chided, smiling as he turned back to the stove.

"How 'bout some flapjacks?"

"Comin' right up. Go make yourself comfortable at the table and I'll have 'em for you in a jiffy!"

A short while later, Elly was in the bedroom getting dressed and Reuben sat at the table, sipping his coffee, when there was a rap at the door and he hollered, "C'mon in captain!"

The door opened and the captain stuck his head in, "Is that coffee I smell?"

"It is, have a seat and I'll pour you a cup," answered Reuben, standing and going to the stove. As the captain seated himself, Reuben poured the coffee and sat down, looked at the officer and said, "I reckon you want that report I promised?"

"Yeah, I was hopin' your wife was doin' better, but I thought it'd be easier for me to come to you." He reached for his cup, took a sip, and set it down, lifted his eyes to Reuben, "But there's something you should know before you begin." He paused a moment before continuing, "President Lincoln has been assassinated!"

Reuben frowned, leaned forward, "Assassinated? By whom, and when?"

"Some actor named Booth, it was shortly after Lee surrendered, and right after you left. But the war's not over. There's still some fighting goin' on, but I think it'll be over soon." He leaned back with the cup in both hands, "Now, tell me 'bout your survey of the area."

Reuben chuckled, "Didn't get to see much. We were lookin' for the camp of the Mouache, finally found it back in the San Juans, but there was a bit of a problem with some gold hunters." He sipped his coffee and continued with the report of seeing the group of prospectors, searching for Kaniache, finding the village and the confrontation with the white men that resulted in Elly's getting wounded. "That same bunch had captured Kaniache's son, Running Elk, and the chief was understandably fightin' mad about that. We asked him to let us see about gettin' his son back from the gold hunters, but they ambushed us. Kaniache was followin' and after Elly was wounded, the last we saw of him, he and his war party were in pursuit of the captors of his son." He paused, sipped his coffee, and shook his head, "I wouldn't wanna be them when he catches up with 'em."

"And there was nothing you could do to stop him?"

"If it was your son, would anything stop you?"

"No, I s'pose not. But that sure doesn't help the peace situation any. You saw the encampment of the Tabeguache and Chief Ouray?"

"Quite a camp it is too. Any progress on a treaty?" asked Reuben.

"Ouray wants peace, that's why he's here. He's willing to give up any claim on the valley, go to a reservation, just not Bosque Redondo. They're not too friendly with the Navajo."

"Well, Kaniache is not too interested in peace like Ouray. He's none too happy with Ouray wanting to give away the valley and he's not happy with the land already seceded. He told me he wants to reclaim all the land that was the home of the Ute people. I kinda think he's about to start a bit of a war with the white man to chase 'em off and reclaim their territory."

"Any idea how he'll go about it?"

"Dunno. He might try to rally some of the other bands, the Caputa, Weeminuche, maybe come here to the Tabeguache. At least, that's what I'd do, but he's a cagey rascal and might just take off on his own with *his* people. He's got maybe a hundred warriors, maybe more. From where he's at, he could swing south, gain some followers from the Caputa, raid across the northern part of *Nuevo México,* maybe come back north, because he sees this land and all the mountains as their historical territory."

The captain shook his head, "That's a lot of territory, and I have less than half the complement of troops for this unit. Even now, Lieutenant Jacobs has a company out on patrol. I told him to look for you and any settlers that might be in trouble or likely to get into trouble, then return to the fort. I expect him back soon, if he doesn't run into Kaniache."

"Let's hope he doesn't," suggested Reuben, leaning back with his coffee in hand. He looked up as Elly came from the bedroom and the captain and Reuben rose to their feet.

The captain spoke, "Good morning, Mrs. Grundy! Good to see you up and about, doing well I presume?"

"Much better captain. Thanks to my husband and the good doctor for taking care of me. I'm still a bit sore, got a ways to go 'fore I'm fit, but I'm making progress, thank you." She fetched herself a cup for coffee, poured it full and set it on the table, offered to refill the men's cups and they all sat down. "Please, continue. Don't let me stifle the conversation."

Reuben chuckled as he was seated, looked at his bride and said, "Just reportin' on our trip and talkin' 'bout Kaniache and what he might do. Oh, and also, the captain tells me that President Lincoln has been assassinated."

"No," she declared, frowning, and looking from Reuben to the captain.

"Yes ma'am. Sad to say, but it happened shortly after the two of you left on your survey."

The genial conversation continued for a short while

until the captain dismissed himself to return to his duties and Reuben and Elly took their refilled cups to the chairs on the stoop to enjoy the morning. They passed the next few days, leisurely enjoying the company of the soldiers, and the pleasant weather that aided in Elly's recovery, until they saw the bedraggled troops riding into the fort, dusty and tired, but with two men that were neither soldiers nor captives.

They watched as the lieutenant went to the commandant's office to report and saw the two men dismount and seat themselves on the boardwalk in front of the sutler's. Reuben frowned, looking from one to the other, but they were not close enough to recognize the two, but he suspicioned he might have seen them before.

The orderly from the commandant's office trotted up to the officer's quarters and stood before Reuben and Elly. "Sir! The captain would like you to come to his office, at once, sir!"

Reuben chuckled, shook his head, and looked at Elly, "It appears I've been summoned." He handed her his cup, rose, and motioned to the orderly to lead the way, and with a glance over his shoulder to his smiling wife, he followed the man back to the captain's office. With a nod and a motion from the orderly, Reuben stepped into the captain's office, saw the dusty lieutenant seated near the window and at the captain's motion, took the chair before the desk.

"Good of you to come, Reuben." He nodded to the junior officer, "You remember the lieutenant, don't you?"

"I do!" replied Reuben, looking to the man, "Mornin' lieutenant." The junior officer nodded, looked back to the captain, and waited for his commander to explain.

"The lieutenant picked up a couple men on his patrol. They were both in bad shape, still are, and had quite a story to tell. I think these are the same ones you encountered, but what they're saying differs a little. They claimed they were attacked by the Ute, two of their men were killed, these two were captured but escaped. They were barefoot, had only strips of trousers on them, had been without food a few days and were headed this way when the patrol picked 'em up."

Reuben lifted his eyebrows at the story, "They probably don't know we're here. It might be a good idea to have one or both of 'em here while we question them. If they're part of the same group, they're guilty of breaking the treaty and going into the Mouache territory uninvited. And taking Kaniache's son captive, well, I'm surprised they're still alive, but I'm sure there's more to the story."

The captain looked at the lieutenant. "Bring 'em in, Jacobs."

The two men were in borrowed bits of clothing and were dirty and disheveled and looked around at the seated men. The fear that showed in their eyes reminded Reuben of the look in the eyes of a captured animal. He nodded to them, and the captain began, "Be seated," motioning to the chairs along the near wall, "Tell us your story, how you ended up in your condition."

"I'm Sean McTavish, and this is my cousin, Aiden McIntyre. We joined up with some men in Fairplay and since all the good claims were taken, we decided to come south. Patrick, that's Patrick Matthews, he had him a map of this country and claimed to know where there was gold. So, we came with him. But when we were followin' the map and tryin' to pan a few streams, those Indians come down on us, killed two of our men, and took the rest of us captive. They tortured Patrick and

Smitty to death, and we escaped, and the lieutenant found us after we'd been walkin' for three days."

The captain looked at Reuben and the lieutenant. "And tell me, Lieutenant Jacobs, where did you find these men?"

"At the mouth of the Rio Grande, sir, there where it comes into the valley. They were in bad shape, delirious, stumbling and staggering around, wavin' and hollerin'. They must have seen us 'fore we saw them."

"Reuben?"

Reuben let a slow grin split his face as he turned to the men, "Now, let me see if I have this straight. The Indians attacked you, killed two of your men, and took you captive. That about it?"

"Yessir, that's right," answered Sean, frowning.

"Didn't you forget a bit of the story, you know, the part about you taking the chief Kaniache's son captive? And the part about you shooting an Indian and a deputy when you ambushed the marshal and shot his wife and the Indian scout? Or the part about you running from the Mouache before they captured you and took back his son?"

Both men fidgeted in their seats, looked frantically at one another, and back at Reuben, "H...H...How'd you know about that?" pleaded Sean.

"I'm the deputy!" snarled Reuben, showing his badge to the men.

31 / REPORTS

The captain looked at the two cousins, frowned and asked, "Now, do you want to amend your story?"

Sean looked to his cousin and at the slight nod, he turned back to the captain, "Yessir." He dropped his eyes, glanced to Reuben, and looked at the captain, "What I said about Fairplay, Patrick and the map, that's all true. And the Indians did attack us, but we fought 'em off, killed a couple. Then we kept goin' into the mountains, the map of Patrick's was a French map that told of a treasure of gold found by some ancient expedition. That's what we were lookin' for, the treasure, and we were getting close! But the Indians struck again, after the big storm that blew through, and tried to steal our horses. That's when the chief's son fell under a horse and broke his leg. Patrick showed him the map and asked if he knew where the waterfall was and he said he did, so Patrick said we should keep him, make him guide us to the falls. That's where we were headed when you," nodding to Reuben, "came up the trail. Patrick was sure you were with the Indians and would keep us from the treasure and he was determined to find it. When you rode up, that Indian lifted his rifle and I thought he was gonna shoot, so I shot him. That's when Smitty shot from below and hit your deputy. But we didn't know you were deputies!" he pleaded, shaking his head. "Then we took off and later on the Indians caught us. The chief's son said we," nodding to his cousin, "treated him right. I splinted his leg for him. But the other two, Patrick and Smitty, they had him hog-tied and roughed him up, so, they were tied to a tree and the women tortured 'em somethin' fierce. I'm sure they killed 'em. But the chief had me'n Aiden run through a gauntlet of women and they whupped on us, boy did they! But he said if we made it through, we could leave. But they took our boots and shirts, gave us one knife, and chased us outta there." He looked to the lieutenant. "It was a couple days later when you found us, and we had about given up. Couldn't catch nuthin', couldn't find anything to eat, we was starvin' and hurtin' and cold…" He shivered at the memory and looked to the floor.

They were interrupted by a rap on the door and the captain responded, "Enter!" The orderly stepped in and handed a paper to the captain, "A telegram from Agent Carson, sir."

The captain frowned, read the telegram, looked up at Reuben and to the two men. "Looks like you've done it!" shaking his head in disgust.

He looked to Reuben and read the gram.

Kaniache of the Mouache stopped here, taking his people to Cimarron. Said he wants peace, but I do not believe it. Have received reports of his raids from Tierra Amarilla to Abiquiu and Ojo Caliente. Probably more. Has four hundred lodges, includes some Caputa. Taking everything from ranches. Believe Jicarilla will join him. Sending gram to Fort Lyon.

"Sounds to me like he's doing what you said. That means he would have twice as many warriors as we have troops, and that includes those at Fort Lyon," growled the captain.

"I don't think you can count on help from Fort Lyon, they've got their hands busy after Sand Creek with Cheyenne, Arapaho, Kiowa, and even some Sioux!" declared Reuben.

The captain looked at the cousins, glanced to the junior officer, "Lieutenant, get these men out of my sight! Put 'em in the guardhouse!"

The lieutenant jumped to his feet, saluted, "Yessir! Right away, sir!" and turned on his heel, motioned to the two men, and followed them out of the office.

"What're you gonna do with them, captain?" asked Reuben.

"That depends on you, Reuben. Even though it's a breach of the treaty for them to go into Indian territory, by law, there's really no punishment I can hand out. Usually we just send 'em packin'. But since they shot your wife and killed that Indian scout, they could be held for that, but you'd have to make the charges. But where you take 'em to be tried in court, well…" he shrugged.

"Can't you have a military trial?"

"Could, but it's really a civil issue."

"What do you recommend?"

"Send 'em packin'. After what Kaniache did, I don't think they'll be interested in goin' back. And, he said it was one of the others that shot your wife."

"But how are they gonna leave? They don't have anything, and it doesn't look like they have any money to get outfitted."

"We can outfit 'em from the sutler, get 'em some horses and show 'em the road!"

"What if..." began Reuben, leaning forward on the captain's desk, and began to lay out a plan of prosecuting the offenders, but getting the result they wanted.

The captain grinned, leaned back in his chair, and put his hands together, tips of each finger touching the opposing finger as he looked at Reuben. "I like it! We'll do that! First thing tomorrow morning!"

Reuben grinned, nodded, and stood to leave. "We might establish a precedent that could be mighty handy in the days to come. With the war ending, I think there's gonna be a lot of folks comin' west to find 'em a new home and with Kaniache on the rampage, it could get bloody!"

"See you in the morning!" declared the captain, chuckling as he watched Reuben leave.

It was an impressive spectacle that began in the central compound with the assembly of troops standing at attention for the raising of the colors as the bugler played "Reveille." When the flag was high, the lieutenant sounded, "Paaarade rest!" and the men dropped their rifles, butts on the ground, left leg one step to the left, left hand behind their back and right hand with rifle extended to the side. Once in position, the lieutenant turned, saluted the captain, and nodded to the escort of the prisoners to bring them forward.

Sean and Aiden were brought out in shackles, each between two soldiers, and stood in front of the captain who stood before them, looking from one to the other. Reuben and Elly stood to the side of the captain and watched the prisoners as the captain began. With a parchment held before him, he began to read,

Whereas on this date, May 21st, 1865, a military tribunal was convened with Captain Charles Kerber, commandant of Fort Garland, Colorado Territory, presiding.

It is hereby decreed that after hearing the testimony of one Sean McTavish and one Aiden McIntyre regarding their activity of the weeks preceding this tribunal, that they did unlawfully enter the territory of the Ute nation and engage in hostilities with the same. Such hostilities did result in the death of four American citizens and an unknown number of the Mouache Ute people. Said defendants did also engage in an ambush of one Reuben Grundy, a deputy United States Marshal, and one Eleanor Grundy, a deputy United States Marshal, and did shoot and wound deputy Eleanor Grundy. After apprehension by a patrol commanded by Lieutenant Edward Jacobs of Fort Garland, Colorado Territory, said defendants were tried and are found guilty of the crime of assault on an officer of the law, and the crime of entering a protected territory. The sentence of this tribunal is for the defendants to serve ten years' incarceration at hard labor. Such sentence will be suspended if defendants accept banishment from Colorado Territory for the remainder of their natural life, unless or until the sentence shall be commuted by proper authority.

Be it so known and carried out as testament by the undersigned authority.

Captain Charles Kerber, commanding, Fort Garland, Colorado Territory.

Deputy Marshal Reuben Grundy, Colorado Territory, United States Marshal Service.

Captain Kerber lowered the parchment and looked at the two men. Sean pleaded, "But captain, we don't have anything! We can't leave here!"

"You will be outfitted by the sutler and there will be horses provided. You have twelve hours to take your leave. If you are still here after that time, you will be thrown into the stockade and serve the minimum sentence of ten years as stipulated by the tribunal."

"Oh, we'll go! Yessir!" responded Sean, looking to his cousin Aiden as he nodded his head in agreement. The captain motioned to the men guarding the prisoners and they set about removing the shackles. As soon as they were freed, the men ran to the sutler's to get the promised gear and get into some new clothes. It was less than an hour and the men were seen riding from the fort, kicking their horses up to a canter, and left without turning back. Reuben looked at the captain who stood beside him in front of the sutler's and chuckled, "Looks like that got rid of 'em!" he declared as the captain laughed at the antics of the two men.

32 / RESOLUTION

Elly put on a fresh pot of coffee and sat down at the table with Reuben. She reached for his hand and asked, "So, what's next?"

He grinned, took her hand in his, "I thought we might take another exploratory journey. We've only seen some of the southernmost part of the valley, so I thought we oughta go north. The captain said they've had settlers, gold hunters, and even trappers that come in from the north end of the valley," he shrugged and started to say more but was interrupted by a knock on the door. "It's open!" he called, looking back at Elly with a smile.

The captain and lieutenant were both at the door and came in at Reuben's call, "Afternoon, ma'am," said the captain, nodding to Elly as he removed his hat. The lieutenant followed his commander's example, nodded, and removed his hat before they accepted Reuben's invitation and took the two remaining seats at the table. Elly rose, took two more cups from the top of the stove's warming oven, and sat them before the visitors to pour them full of steaming coffee.

"So, what's next for you two?" asked the captain, enjoying his first sip of coffee.

"That's what we were just starting to talk about captain. Considering taking another look-see and go north along the east edge of the valley. That way we can see if there's any activity in the mountains, swing across the north end like you showed us, and come back south along the west side," answered Reuben.

"Sounds reasonable," interjected the lieutenant, not to be left out of the conversation.

"The west side is Caputa Ute country. The Tabeguache were usually in the northwest. But there's no tellin' where you'll find settlers and gold hunters," explained the captain.

"That's kinda what I thought. But that'd give us a better understanding of the country, maybe meet some new folks, both native and settlers." Reuben paused, took a sip of coffee, and looked at Jacobs, "Lieutenant, when you took that patrol out, did you run into a group of settlers, two wagons, three men, two women, and some youngsters?"

The junior officer dropped his head, sighed, and looked up at Reuben, "We did. They had a run-in with some natives, Apache, I think. Wagons burnt, no survivors. We buried their remains. They were sorta dressed alike, men had black trousers, blue shirts, and women had the same color dresses, at least from what we could tell," he was frowning, shook his head slightly at the memory and looked up at Reuben. "Did you know them?"

"Met 'em. They camped near us the last night on the trail. I think they were Quakers."

"Quakers? Never heard of 'em. What are they?"

"It's a religious group, good folks, believe 'bout the same as we do," nodding to his wife.

"And what's that?" asked the captain.

"Well, let me ask *you* a question. Your occupation is sort of a dangerous one and I'm sure you've given some thought to this. If you were to die today, do you know for sure that you'd go to Heaven?" He paused, looking from the captain to the lieutenant and let the question hang in the silence for a moment. "I'm guessing by your silence you've thought about that but not come up with an answer. Am I right?"

"You're right. And like most soldiers, I've thought about it but without a good answer, I try *not* to think about it. You know, I reckon I'm like most people, figger if I do good, be a good man, you know, then that'll get me there. I consider myself a good man and try to do my best."

"What about you, Jacobs?"

"I've never given it much thought. My pa always said, 'when you're dead, you're dead!' and I didn't think much about it. But now that you ask the question, is there an answer?"

"It's what I learned as a young man, before I went to war. My pa set me down in the barn one day and we had a serious talk. Oh, we had gone to church, whenever they had services and there was a preacher come by, but just listenin' to some old man standin' up and shoutin' about sin, well, I never paid much attention. But Pa, he knew the good book, and he set me down and showed me what I needed to do, so, I'm gonna share that with you men because I believe it's the most important decision you'll ever make in your lifetime." He looked from one to the other, each man nodding and scooting to the edge of their seat as they leaned their elbows on the table, cradling the coffee in both hands.

Reuben had his Bible on the table and began leafing through the pages and stopped at I John 5:13 and began reading, *These things have I written unto you that believe on the name of the Son of God..."* Reuben looked at both men and asked, "You believe in Jesus, don't you?"

"Yes, yes, I do. I don't know much but I know that," answered the captain.

Reuben looked at Jacobs who responded, "That's just it. I don't know much about him. Oh, I've heard talk about him and such, but..." and shrugged.

"I understand. But this is the Word of God, and He says He has written these things for a reason and that reason is...*that ye may know that ye have eternal life, and that ye may believe on the name of the Son of God.* It's so we can *know* eternal life and that we *may believe* on Him. To have eternal life is to live forever or for eternity, and that is certainly not to live forever here on earth, it's to have eternal life in Heaven forever. And He tells us how, you see He makes it simple in the book of Romans and He basically lays out four things we need to know."

As he spoke, he turned the pages of the Bible and stopped at Romans chapter three. "Now the first thing is here in verse 10. *As it is written, there is none righteous, no, not one.* And he also says it in verse 23. *For all have sinned and come short of the glory of God.* It tells us that we're all sinners, you understand that, don't you?" he asked, looking from one to the other. Both men nodded, the captain raised his eyebrows as he nodded his agreement. "And it also says we've *come short of the glory of God.* That simply means because we're sinners, we miss out on Heaven.

"But, the second thing kinda adds to that, because

we're sinners, there's a penalty. In 6:23 He says, *For the wages of sin is death;* which tells us the penalty—death and hell forever. But He doesn't want us to have to go there and He promises more, *but the gift of God is eternal life through Jesus Christ our Lord.* So, the second thing we need to know is, there's a penalty of death hanging over us because we're sinners. But the third thing we need to know is God has a gift for us, and that gift is eternal life —to live in Heaven for all eternity and it's a free gift! *But* that gift is through Jesus Christ our Lord.

"See, like any gift, it had to be paid for, and Jesus did just that. He paid for it on the cross when he was crucified. The penalty for sin is death, so in 5:8 *But God commendeth* or showed *His love toward us, in that while we were yet sinners,* now this is the most important part, *Christ died for us.* See there, that gift through Jesus was paid for by Him on the cross. He died for us and because He died, that paid the price for our free gift of eternal life."

Reuben paused, took a drink of coffee, and looked at the men who were still leaning forward, watching and listening. "Now, like any gift, it doesn't do any good just sitting there, it must be received. So, He even tells us how to do that. In chapter ten beginning at verse 9, He says, *That if thou shalt confess with thy mouth the Lord Jesus, and shalt believe in thine heart that God hath raised him from the dead, thou shalt be saved. For with the heart man believeth unto righteousness; and with the mouth confession is made unto salvation.* Verse 13, *For whosoever shall call upon the name of the Lord shall be saved.* It's as simple as that. If we believe in our hearts—not just a belief in our minds," he tapped his forehead, "that it's true, but in our hearts," he held his clenched fist at his heart as he looked at the men. "Believe here, and ask Him for the gift, and it's ours. He says when we do that, we will be saved. Saved from what? Saved from eternal hell and given the free gift of eternal life, to live forever in Heaven."

"So, how do we do that?" asked the captain.

Reuben smiled, "You just asked me a question, or you 'called upon' me. That's how we do it. We simply ask Him for that free gift. When we pray, we admit we're sinners and knowing the penalty for that sin, we ask Him for His gift of eternal life. And He never says no." He looked from one to the other, "If you'd like to do that right now, I can lead us in prayer, show you what to do, and we can get it done right now. Would you like to do that?"

The men looked at each other, back to Reuben and both nodded their heads in agreement. Reuben also nodded, dropped his head, and began, "Dear God…" and continued in prayer thanking Him for His Word and His promise. Then with his head still bowed, he spoke to the men. "Now if you want to receive that free gift and you believe with all your heart, and don't do it unless you truly believe, then repeat this prayer after me." He paused, giving them a moment to consider and decide, then continued, "Dear God…I know I'm a sinner…and I ask for forgiveness…and I believe with my heart…what your word says…and I ask for that gift…of eternal life… come into my heart…and save me…thank you…in Jesus name…amen."

The men, with voices low, had repeated the words and as they said 'Amen' they lifted their eyes to Reuben, both smiling and Reuben shook their hands and said, "Amen!"

Elly smiled and fetched the coffee pot, refilling each man's cup and her own, then returned the pot and sat down. "So, now that we got you settled about where you're going," she nodded to the men, and looked at her husband, "and we know *we're* going to Heaven. But where are we going now?"

Everyone chuckled, relaxed, and the captain said, "You know, since you're going north, there's a hot springs up thataway. I'm bettin' that hot pool would feel mighty good on your wound."

"Ummm, that does sound inviting. You're gonna hafta tell us exactly where it is, I don't want to miss out on that!"

33 / DIRECTION

It was a clear day, the sun was bright, the azure sky arched overhead with nary a cloud, and Bear led the way. He was excited to be back on the trail, so much so he would run ahead, jump high and twist around before landing, turning to face the slow pokes following and with tongue lolling, his eyes exclaimed, "Hurry up! We're burnin' daylight!"

Elly chuckled at the antics of her big dog, looked to Reuben at her side and said, "He's gonna want to get in that hot springs before us!"

"Probably. But we've got lots of time, no hurry. There's also a nice cold waterfall up here a little ways that'll make for a nice coolin' off."

"Brrr, I think I like the idea of hot springs better."

The sun was high, and the day turned warm when they ducked into the edge of the tree line to follow a trail that pointed to a long cut in the mountains of the Sangre de Cristo Range. The trail sided a creek that chuckled over the rocks, often splashing and crashing as the steep foothill caused a cascade of white water. The deep shadows of the thick timber parted and showed a cluster of white-barked aspen surrounding a clearing of deep grass. They stepped down, loosened the girths on the horses and mule and Reuben began fetching some firewood for a fresh pot of coffee. There was an older fire ring with black charcoal and grey ashes that told of earlier travelers and Elly began building a small fire.

They enjoyed their midday repast and stretched out in the shade of the aspen on the upper end of the clearing. The horses were grazing in the flat at the high end as well, until Bear came to all fours, looking downhill and growling. Elly and Reuben sat up, looking where Bear was pointed and watched, Reuben grabbing up his Henry without taking his eyes off the lower end of the clearing. It looked like the shadows were moving when a ball of fur bounded into the clearing and slid to a stop, staring up at all the animals on the upper end of the clearing.

The cinnamon bear cub had everyone's attention. Even the horses had turned, standing tall with ears pricked, nostrils flaring and eyes wide. The smell of bear struck fear into each one, but Bear had stopped growling, watched the playful furball, and took a couple steps toward him. The cub had dropped to his haunches, cocked his head to one side and looked at everyone. Elly whispered, "Ahhh, it's just a cub! Not more'n a couple weeks old. But where's his mama?"

"That's what the rest of us are wonderin'," answered Reuben slowly coming to his feet, trying his best to see into the shadowy black timber below them. He glanced down to see Bear slowly moving toward the cub, his tail wagging and his jowls drooling. As Reuben jacked a cartridge into the chamber, slowly and quietly, Elly worked her way to her appaloosa, Daisy, to retrieve her rifle from the scabbard. She kept watching the bear cub who cocked his head from one side to the other, curious about these new creatures. With rifle in hand, she also slowly jacked a cartridge into the chamber and moved back near Reuben.

Bear neared the cub, stopped, and dropped to his haunches. The cub had been watching him closely and when he stopped, the cub came to all fours and slowly picked his way closer. As he neared, he reached out his nose and the two touched noses, sniffing and searching. At first contact, they both jerked back, then slowly reached forward again. It was easy to see them both relax, almost smile, and start examining one another, nose to tail. The cub, satisfied with his new discovery, turned away, looked back over his shoulder as if inviting Bear to follow and the two scampered into the woods. Bear barked as he ran after the smaller cub but had shown no fear. They could be heard, Bear barking, the cub squealing, as they bounded in and out among the trees. Within moments, they came bounding back into the clearing, ran out the other side, and disappeared again.

Reuben and Elly were so intent on watching the two cavort, they did not notice, until the horses snorted and stirred, the presence of the big mama bear at the lower end of the clearing as she rose up on hind legs, front legs pawing the air and let loose a leaf-rattling roar. Reuben and Elly both brought their rifles around to take aim on the big bear, but the cub and dog came crashing through, still cavorting in their play and almost knocked the mama bear down. She dropped to all fours, growled at her cub who twisted around to look at her, and with head down, slowly walked to his mama. She growled at him, apparently scolding the recalcitrant cub, swatted him on the rump as he passed by and without a glance to the creatures at the upper end of the clearing, mama and cub disappeared into the trees, leaving a disappointed big dog behind. Bear looked up at Elly, back to the trees where his new friend had disappeared, and trotted up to see Elly and get some loving.

Bear was not disappointed. Elly and Reuben returned the rifles to the scabbards, stretched out on the tall grass in the shade of the aspen, and Bear lay his head on Elly's midriff as she began petting and talking to him. Reuben grinned at the pair, "You should be scolding him for not protecting us! After all, he did let a bear come into our camp without warning," he chuckled.

"He knew we didn't need protecting. Didn't you boy," she answered as she stroked the big dog's broad head. "You know, that's why I never want to leave the mountains. Where else could we have an experience like that?"

"Just about anywhere there's bears, I suppose," answered Reuben.

"Oh, come on, you've never seen a cinnamon bear anywhere but here in these mountains. And to have a cub playin' with your dog, that's special! But that's not all, we've seen so many of God's amazing creatures, met more natives than most folks believe even exist, and seen more of God's creation than we ever imagined." She shook her head, "Nope, ain't never gonna leave!"

"Sounds good to me! Now, you want a cold shower under that waterfall or you gonna wait for the hot springs?"

"See, no matter where we go, there are wonders to behold. Either His handiwork in creation, or His blessings in the wonders of the animal kingdom."

Reuben sat up, frowning, and quietly went to the horses to retrieve his Henry. He walked back to Elly's side, glanced down to see her frowning at him, and with a nod and a whisper, "We got company! Two-legged this time. Walking through the trees, yonder." He watched a moment, frowning, "Whoever it is, he's either hurt or doesn't know his way around the woods." He stepped to the side, leaned over a bit more to see through the trees, and said, "Get your rifle, cover me."

Elly jumped to her feet and in three long strides was at the side of her appy, slipping the Henry from the scabbard. She turned to see Reuben move into the trees, and the shadows seemed to envelope him. She took a few steps forward, moving side to side to try to see, and Reuben came into the clearing, his arm around a man, helping him toward their camp. A mop of grey hair obscured the face of the man whose head hung down, but his bare arms and torso showed leathery skin, and fringed buckskin leggings and moccasins said he was a native, but nothing told what tribe.

Reuben lowered him to a rock beside the fire pit where embers still glowed and the man rested elbows on his knees, slowly lifted his wrinkled face to look at Elly. A smile showed few teeth, but his eyes danced with life and mischief. Elly smiled, nodded, and said, "Welcome to our camp."

She looked up at Reuben, "See, there's always something that keeps things interesting! Don't you just love these mountains?" she giggled as she rose to get a cup to give the man some coffee.

With a combination of sign language, English, and a few words of Shoshonean, they soon understood his name was Crooked Nose and he had been a war leader of the Comanche. His woman and son had been taken by the smallpox, and he had come to the mountains to die. But he was thinking about returning to his people, join the council of elders and share his wisdom but had grown weak with nothing to eat.

"The Comanche are in the mountains, southeast of Fort Garland. You're a long ways from your people."

"I can make it if I have something to eat," he stated.

Reuben grinned, saw the man had a knife in a sheath at his waist, and went to the fresh carcass of the deer taken that morning and cut a big chunk from the hind quarter and dropped it on the rock beside the man. He looked up at Reuben, grinned his almost toothless grin, and nodded. He finished his coffee and the last of the corn dodgers. With a smile to Elly and a nod of thanks to Reuben, he put the meat across his shoulder and stood and walked from the camp looking more like a young man than the oldster he was—with a fresh spring in his step and hope in his heart.

Elly looked at Reuben, smiled and broke into laughter, prompted Reuben to do the same and as they tightened the girths on their horses, they continued to chuckle at the old man that had walked away with a good meal, fresh meat, and renewed hope, all because he met these two people. As they swung aboard, they pointed the horses north along a faint trail that cut through the timber and dropped to the edge of the trees, shouldering the foothills of the Sangre de Cristo Mountains.

It was a beautiful land, green fertile soil watered by many runoff streams from the high country that skirted the black timbered shoulders of the magnificent mountains. Stretching out westward was the wide flat and sometimes rolling plains of the San Luis Valley, covered with buffalo grass, gramma, sage brush, greasewood, and a variety of cacti. Beyond the plains stood the misty image of the San Juan Mountains, the land of mystery and wonders, the home of many different bands of the Ute people.

Reuben reined up as they crested a long rise that extended into the valley from the higher mountains and offered an unparalleled vista of the countryside. He leaned on the pommel of his saddle, admiring the panorama as Elly came alongside. "Beautiful, isn't it?" her voice soft with wonder and love.

"Ummhmm. Can't ever get tired of all this!" he declared.

"Don't want to either. But there's a hot springs that's calling me and we won't get there till next week at this pace."

Reuben looked at her, grinned, and mumbled, "Women! Always in a hurry!" and nudged Blue back to the trail, motioned to Bear to scout ahead, and smiled back at Elly, "Well, you comin'?" he chuckled, laughing as she slapped legs to the appaloosa to catch up.

TAKE A LOOK AT: ROCKY MOUNTAIN SAINT

THE COMPLETE CHRISTIAN MOUNTAIN MAN SERIES

Best-selling western author B.N. Rundell takes you on a journey through the wilderness in this complete 14-book mountain man saga!

Holding on to the dream of living in the Rocky Mountains that Tatum shared with his father, he begins his journey—a journey that takes him through the lands of the Osage and Kiowa and ultimately to the land of the Comanche. Now he has a family, and the wilderness makes many demands on anyone that tries to master the mountains...

"Rundell's Rocky Mountain Saint series is marvelous and inspiring." **– Reader**

Follow Tate Saint, man of the mountains, on his journey from boyhood to manhood where he faces everything from the wilds of the wilderness to forces of nature and historic wars.

Rocky Mountain Saint: The Complete Series includes – Journey to Jeopardy, Frontier Freedom, Wilderness Wanderin', Mountain Massacre, Timberline Trail, Pathfinder Peril, Wapiti Widow, Vengeance Valley, Renegade Rampage, Buffalo Brigade, Territory Tyranny, Winter Waifs, Mescalero Madness and Dine' Defiance.

AVAILABLE NOW

ABOUT THE AUTHOR

Born and raised in Colorado into a family of ranchers and cowboys, **B.N. Rundell** is the youngest of seven sons. Juggling bull riding, skiing, and high school, graduation was a launching pad for a hitch in the Army Paratroopers. After the army, he finished his college education in Springfield, MO, and together with his wife and growing family, entered the ministry as a Baptist preacher.

Together, B.N. and Dawn raised four girls that are now married and have made them proud grandparents. With many years as a successful pastor and educator, he retired from the ministry and followed in the footsteps of his entrepreneurial father and started a successful insurance agency, which is now in the hands of his trusted nephew. He has also been a successful audiobook narrator and has recorded many books for several award-winning authors. Now finally realizing his life-long dream, B.N. has turned his efforts to writing a variety of books, from children's picture books and young adult adventure books, to the historical fiction and western genres which are his first love.

Made in the USA
Middletown, DE
08 November 2023

42186265R00136